~~MERRY~~ *Creepy* CHRISTMAS

12 Twisted Tales

2022

FROM BLACK MARE BOOKS

Contents

THOUGH THE FROST WAS CRUEL— 1
By Artemis Greenleaf

WHILE MORTALS SLEEP— 10
By A.B. Richards

DO YOU SEE WHAT I SEE— 17
By Holly Dey

IT CAME UPON A MIDNIGHT CLEAR— 24
By A.B. Richards

DREAMING OF A WHITE CHRISTMAS— 35
By Artemis Greenleaf

A CHRISTMAS COYOTE— 42
By A.B. Richards

OH, TANNENBAUM— 51
By Artemis Greenleaf

A WHIP THAT CRACKS— 62
By Artemis Greenleaf

ONE HORSE OPEN SLAY— 70
By A.B. Richards

STALKING IN A WINTER WONDERLAND— 76
By Holly Dey

THE SILENT STARS GO BY— 86
By A.B. Richards

SAD TIDINGS WE BRING— 97
By A.B. Richards

Though The Frost Was Cruel

By Artemis Greenleaf

D o we really have to go to your mother's?" Diane laid a hand on her protruding belly.

"It's Christmas," Mel replied, setting his mug down on the coffee table. "We always go on Christmas."

"I'm not usually eight and a half months pregnant at Christmas. I'm tired, my feet are swollen, and my back hurts. I just want to sleep. She's had five children—surely, she'll understand."

Mel pouted. "Ft. Worth isn't *that* far from Mother's house. And I'll be driving. You can sleep in the car."

"You know I have to pee every thirty minutes. And it's supposed to snow. What if I go into labor?"

"You might be surprised to learn they have hospitals in Lubbock."

Diane pressed her lips together. "A strange hospital and a doctor that doesn't know me. Sounds fun."

He reached out and stroked her hair. "Sorry, babe. It's the Imperial Summons, to be ignored on pain of disinheritance. It's only a few days. We'll be back in plenty of time before your due date."

She sighed and went to pack a bag.

"Why? Why, Mel, didn't you get gas at the truck stop back in Abilene?" The car crawled along the desolate highway at forty miles an hour, Mel's strategy for saving enough fuel to get to the next town.

"I'm sorry. Thought we had enough. I just wanted to get back on the road before it got cold enough for the snow to stick. Every pump had a line."

A light glimmered ahead through the wet, clumpy flakes that drifted down on them. They melted as soon as they touched the black asphalt, but the scrubby bushes that spotted the roadside had begun to accumulate a white dusting.

Diane squinted. "What do you suppose that is?" She tugged the seat belt away from her throat. "There haven't been any lights on the highway for a while now."

"Not sure."

The flakes got smaller and drier and fell faster.

Mel pushed the car to forty-five. "I don't want to be on the road if this stuff is going to freeze."

As they got closer, it became clear that the glimmer was a neon sign. Not all of it lit up, but it represented a seven-pointed star with a flashing comet tail, looking as if it had broken down on the side of the road on its way to Vegas and given up its quest in despair. A much smaller rectangular sign further down the pole flashed a glowing green 'V can y.'

Diane grunted. "This baby is doing a gymnastics routine in there. Why don't we see if they have any rooms? We could call for roadside assistance in the morning and I can walk around for a bit. That usually settles him."

"Okay. Probably best to get off the road, anyway."

The car limped into the rugged parking lot and Mel pulled up as close to the office door as he could get. He left the car running while he went inside. After a few minutes, he returned, swinging a metal key attached to a large plastic rectangle.

"There's a blast from the past," Diane said. "What room are we in?"

"117. It's on the key ring."

"So it is. Didn't realize anyone still used these."

"Well, the lady at the front desk looked like a refugee from the sixties, so I'm not very surprised it's old school. And you know what else was weird? There was a red jerry can in the lobby. It was full of gas, so I asked if I could buy it off her. Said she'd add it to the bill."

"That's handy. It's really starting to snow hard. Glad we found this place. Hope your mother isn't too angry that we're a day late."

"Me, too. Let's get you inside. Room's just on the end there. I'll come back and get the gas once you're situated."

The footsteps of many years had battered a threadbare path in the wavy, sculpted teal carpet. Mustard yellow curtains matched the quilted bedspreads. Faux wood paneling behind the beds gave the eye scant relief from the busy palm tree wallpaper.

"Home, sweet home." Mel dropped a bag on one of the sagging twin beds. "Back in a few." He kissed Diane's cheek on the way out.

She paced back and forth around the tiny room. After a few minutes, the baby settled, and she went to the bathroom. There was no restaurant at the motel, and the closest town was at least another twenty miles away. Even with a few gallons of gas, she didn't want to venture out into the snowstorm. Diane picked through the bag of road snacks and settled on potato chips.

Mel came back into the room, rubbing his hands together. "That five gallons of gas should easily get us to town in the morning." He went to the sink and ran hot water over his stiff fingers.

Diane patted the sack next to her on the bed. "Not much of a supper, but at least we're not stranded on the side of the road somewhere."

His shoulders sagged. "I've let you down again. I'm sorry."

She shrugged. "It's okay. I'm not that hungry, anyway. I am a little crampy, though. I just want to stretch out and get off my feet."

The darkness of the room was shattered by a loud groan.

Mel sat up and snapped on the bedside lamp. "Diane? You okay?"

"No. Help me up. I need to walk."

She paced around the room, grimacing. "I think… I think the baby's coming."

"What?"

"I'm in labor."

He swore and grabbed his jacket. "I'll get help."

Mel ran to the front office. When he returned with the clerk, his wife was nowhere to be seen.

"Diane! Where are you?" He flung open the bathroom door to find her standing in the tub in a puddle of water. "Are you… taking a shower? Now?"

"No, you idiot. My water just broke," she snapped.

"Sorry. The phone lines are down and I can't get a cell signal. But Linda here can help."

Diane eyed the clerk. Linda was young, college aged. She had the biggest hair Diane had seen since that photo of her mom and friends from the eighties, and she looked warm in a boxy, lime green winter coat that completely obscured her figure.

"Ooooooohh," Diane grunted as another contraction hit her. "Now what?"

A pink blush was spreading over the eastern horizon when Bryan let out his first cry. Linda wrapped him in a towel and handed him to Mel. She waited a few minutes, then severed the umbilical cord and knotted it. Mel placed the baby on Diane's chest.

Linda smiled from underneath her bouffant, the bow still perfectly in place. "There's a clinic in town—they should be able to check you out. Stay on Highway 84. It'll be just inside the city limits. You can't miss it."

"Thanks." Diane was exhausted, but there was no rest for her in the run-down motel room. She needed medical attention, ASAP.

"I have a few baby things. Just give me a minute."

Linda left. By the time she returned, Mel had packed up the few items they'd brought in from the car.

Linda handed over two cloth diapers with a plastic diaper cover, a long-sleeved onesie, and a baby quilt.

Diane ran her fingers over the blanket. "Is this handmade? It's very distinctive."

Linda nodded.

"We can't take this. It must be really special to you."

"You can't take Bryan out in the snow with no coat or anything. It's fine. My mom can make another one. Really. She loves to sew."

"Thank you. I don't know what we would have done if you hadn't been here."

Mel bit his lip. "You don't happen to have a baby seat we could borrow, do you?"

"Baby seat?"

"You know, for the car?"

Linda shook her head. "Sorry, I don't."

"It's okay. We really appreciate everything you've done for us." Mel gave her a haggard smile.

"Glad I could help. Drive safely."

Mel carried Bryan to the car. Diane was walking, but shaky and feeling somewhat unstable. Once she was buckled in, he handed the baby over.

They were halfway to town when Mel slapped his forehead with the palm of his hand. "I forgot to pay for the room."

"We can't turn around and do it now. We have to get to the clinic first."

"You're right."

There were a few cars in the parking lot of the urgent care clinic. Mel parked and helped Diane and the baby out of the car. She sat in a chair near the front desk while Mel checked them in. Bryan slept, and Diane shifted around in the seat, trying to find a position that didn't hurt.

An old woman glared at her from across the small waiting room. Diane looked away and fidgeted with the edge of the quilt. The rattle of a walker on the hardwood floor made her look up.

The woman stopped close in front of Diane, nearly running over her foot with a front wheel. "Where did you get that?" she demanded.

"Get what? The baby?" Diane didn't have the energy to deal with nosy strangers at the moment.

The old woman pointed a clawed hand at the blanket. "Don't play dumb with me. That quilt. Where did you get it?"

"Not that it's any of your business, but the lady at the motel gave it to us."

"The motel!" The crone scowled. "What motel?"

Diane leaned back in her seat, clutching Bryan a little tighter. "What does it matter to you?"

"My mother made that quilt for my sister many years ago. How did you get it?"

"I told you. The lady at the motel gave it to us. Now, if you'll please stop crowding me?"

The woman took a step back but leaned forward on her walker. "What motel?"

Diane looked over her shoulder toward Mel. He was still filling out forms. "If you must know, it was The Star Motel."

Her eyes filling with tears, the woman leaned on her walking frame. After she took a moment to compose herself, she pulled a heavy locket from her blouse and opened it, shoving the faded photo in Diane's face.

Bryan stirred and Diane repositioned him. "That's Linda. She works at the motel. Is she your granddaughter?"

The woman put the locket away and blotted her eyes with a tissue pulled from the canvas pouch attached to the front of the walker. "She was my sister."

"I find that hard to believe. No offense, but you've got to be well into your seventies, and Linda can't be older than twenty-five."

"She was twenty-three. Linda was pregnant, less than a month away from having her baby. I told her she shouldn't be working out there in the middle of nowhere and gone, being that far along. She laughed at me and said she didn't need to go into confinement. This was the Space Age, not the Victorian. But a snowstorm hit and knocked out the power. Apparently, she was trying to make a fire to keep warm with some gas from the maintenance building when the motel office caught on fire."

"I'm very sorry to hear about your sister—"

"Diane? They're ready for us."

She looked at Mel and nodded before glancing back at the old woman. "Excuse me."

When she got to the door that led to the treatment rooms, Mel put his hand on her lower back. "What did she want?"

"Oh, she thought she recognized the quilt. Poor thing. Must have dementia."

While Diane was being stitched up, Mel found the big box store and purchased a car seat, diapers, and some warm clothes for Bryan. A nurse wheeled Diane and Bryan to the front door, then came out with them to check the car seat. She tightened the seatbelt and adjusted the tether before allowing Mel to strap a drowsy Bryan into it.

Mel slipped behind the wheel and started the ignition. "Let's go pay Linda before I forget."

"Good plan. You did fill up, didn't you?"

"Of course."

They turned around and headed back down Highway 84. It wasn't long before they were almost to the next town.

"You must have passed it, Mel."

"I would have seen the only building on the road."

He made a U-turn at the city limits sign and drove more slowly on the way back. The thin coat of snow had melted, except for a few shallow drifts in the shade.

After a while, something tall sprouted from the side of the road some way down.

"Must be the sign. Don't know how we missed it before," Mel said.

The rusty pole got closer, and Mel let his foot off the gas. "I don't understand."

He pulled into the parking lot and both of them got out of the car.

The thin rectangle with the broken neon 'Vacancy' dangled by a cable, and the sign for the motel was gone, but the pole still stood in front of the large, empty slab.

While Mortals Sleep

By A.B. Richards

Aunt Matilda leaned over and set some gifts underneath the tree. Her husband—Uncle Martin—had survived the Great War but succumbed to the final wave of the Spanish Flu. She only wore black these days, and her clothes matched her glossy bob. She smiled at her niece before continuing to the dining room.

Chester frowned at these latest additions to the pile of gifts under the Christmas tree. "Your Aunt Matilda is very peculiar."

"Perhaps," Evelyn replied. "But she is a dear. Being unconventional is *not* a crime, especially when she puts such enthusiasm into it."

"Unconventional! Darling, she has a tattoo."

"Only a small one. It's under her clothes—no one would ever see it." Evelyn smoothed her hair. "You know how close she and Philip are. I can't wait to see what she's gotten for him."

"I've half a mind to open it after he's asleep, so I can throw it out if it's wildly inappropriate."

Evelyn poked a finger into his chest. "You will do no such thing! His favorite presents are the ones he gets from her. You'll ruin Christmas for everybody."

He sneered and grabbed her finger. "Give women the right to vote, and they think they own the place."

She pulled back from his loose grip. "President Harding is happy enough about that. Come on. Pour us some of your prescription brandy. Dinner'll be served soon."

Aunt Matilda laid her fork across her plate. "Don't you worry, Philip. The monster under your bed will soon be on the run. I promise."

The little boy gave her a wan smile. He was far too young to have such bags under his eyes, and his cheeks should have been pink and plump, instead of pale and drawn.

Chester set his napkin on the table, pursing his lips. "You shouldn't encourage this nonsense. Monsters do not exist, nor do they habitate underneath beds."

Philip curled into himself. "May I be excused, please?"

The patriarch tapped the table. "Finish your peas first."

The boy drooped, picked up his fork, and began half-heartedly stabbing at the dull green spheres in their congealing puddle of butter sauce.

Matilda's eyes glittered between squinted lids, but she said nothing.

Discomforted by the tension, the rest of the family members drifted away from the table—Evelyn's parents, her sister and brother-in-law, Chester's mother, his two brothers and their wives. It was Chester's house, after all, and not their place to question his authority.

He frowned at his son's progress. "Hurry up, boy, or it's the strap for you."

Tears welled in Philip's eyes as he scooped more peas onto a quaking fork.

"I'm sure the gentlemen are eager for their Christmas Eve card game. I'll sit with him."

"Don't coddle the boy, Evelyn. It'll make him weak, and weak men have no place in this world. I raise him just as my father raised me, so he'll be every bit as strong and successful. You do want that for your son, don't you?"

Evelyn patted her husband's hand. "My sister said that Hermie got his hands on some Cuban cigars."

"Cubans, huh? Hand rolled?"

"Of course."

Chester frowned at his son. "All of the peas." Then he got to his feet and kissed his wife on the top of her head before hurrying off to join the menfolk in the drawing room.

Evelyn moved to sit next to her son. She brushed the white-blond hair from his forehead and smiled at him.

"You need to keep up your strength. You're getting thin."

"Not very hungry."

She looked at the glistening, olive drab peas sprawling on the plate. "The Eversons down the street brought their Christmas card around this afternoon. And a batch of their chef's famous cookies. Do you think you could manage one of those?"

His eyes widened with hope.

"Come on. Bring your plate and let's go to the kitchen."

Evelyn swore her own cook to secrecy, sealing the deal with the gifted sweets, one for the cook and one for her husband. Philip sat at the small table while his mother took a bottle of milk from the icebox and poured him a cup.

She brought a small plate with two more cookies and set the glass next to Philip. "Drink up. Nanny will be looking for you soon to put you to bed. All of your cousins are already asleep."

"They're babies." He took a bite of the orange drop cookie and chewed slowly, as if stretching out the time before he had to go to bed.

Evelyn clasped his wrist and brought it closer to her. "How did you get these scrapes?"

He lowered his head and peered at her from beneath his eyelashes. "Monster."

Her forehead wrinkled. "The monster under your bed did this to you?"

Philip popped the rest of the cookie into his mouth and nodded.

Evelyn leaned back in her chair, gnawing the inside of her cheek, while Philip finished his milk.

"Alright. Upstairs with you. You know your father likes an early Christmas."

The babies, who were far too young to appreciate Christmas traditions, were kept out of sight and earshot by their nannies. Philip would be allowed to open his presents first, so that he could go off and entertain himself while the adults took a more leisurely round-robin approach. Before him lay a pile of die-cast iron animal figures, a pair of roller skates, a scarf, and two books—*The Children of Odin* and *The Velveteen Rabbit*.

Chester eyed Aunt Matilda as he handed Philip the last package. Eagerly, the boy tore off the paper and tugged open the box. He pulled out a handmade teddy bear and held it high. "Thank you, auntie!"

"You are very welcome, Philip. He'll sort that monster right out."

Evelyn recoiled. The teddy bear had a wolfish look to it and felt more dangerous than comforting, with its pointed snout and charcoal fur. The thing's eyes unnerved her the most. Whether they were pressed glass or carved from obsidian, she couldn't say, but they gleamed in the morning light, treacherous as January rain.

A serving girl gathered the other gifts from the floor and carried them away to Philip's playroom as he followed hard on her heels, swinging the uncanny bear.

Chester smirked at Aunt Matilda. "There are no monsters under the bed, but that godawful thing will surely give him nightmares."

"We shall see."

The rest of Christmas day was filled with feasting, proud displays of gifted jewelry, eggnog, and a church service. The gentlemen polished off the brandy before bed and were quite merry before turning in.

Evelyn was awaked by a scream.

Sunlight streamed in from gaps in the draperies, but she jumped out of bed and dashed into the corridor without taking a moment to put on her robe. Chester and one of his brothers stood in the hallway in front of Philip's door. Evelyn's mother comforted a sobbing nanny.

Evelyn ran past them into her son's room.

Philip sat in his bed, rubbing his eyes.

On the expensive rug beneath the bed lay several bloody shreds of fur.

Chester sauntered into the room and lifted a long, hairless tail from the bloody debris. "Well, I suppose there was a monster after all. This is the largest rat I've ever seen. Must be a hole in the baseboard behind the bed. Lucky someone forgot to put the cat out last night."

The eerie stuffed bear lay next to Philip. Its glossy black eyes seemed to stare through Evelyn's very soul.

Aunt Matilda stepped into the room and pulled open the curtains. "See? I told you he'd protect you from monsters."

The adults drifted back to their rooms to dress for the day, leaving the staff to deal with the bloody rodent remains.

✳ ✳ ✳

After the new year, the holiday guests had departed and the household returned to normal. Philip still slept with the Christmas bear and color had returned to his cheeks. Evelyn's worries about him eased.

It was the dead of night when her eyes popped open. She listened in the dark. At first, she heard nothing, then a snarl came from down the hallway. Chester's room was further from the nursery than hers, and Evelyn hoped he'd meet her in the hallway. She crept toward the noise. There was a loud grunt, followed by a thump, and a gurgling began.

The sounds were coming from Philip's room.

Evelyn flung open the door. "Philip!"

The boy sat up in bed. "Mother?"

"What's happening?"

"I don't know. I was sleeping."

A shadow loomed near the end of the bed, and a dark form lay on the floor nearby. She pulled on the cord near Philip's door and a servant appeared as if by magic to light the gas lamp.

Evelyn's hand flew to her mouth and her knees went weak.

Chester lay on the floor in his night clothes. His blank eyes stared at the ceiling—his throat had been ripped out.

"Stay in bed, Philip! Close your eyes."

The boy did as he was told, clutching his teddy to his chest. Its dark fur nestled against his sleeve, leaving a single drop of bright red blood, stark against his snowy nightshirt.

Do You See What I See

By Holly Dey

Amity Hudson scowled at her mail. "Who names their child 'Fontanelle?' Isn't that the soft spot—"

"Ahem."

She whirled to find her next-door neighbor standing even with her in his own drive.

He quirked an eyebrow. "It is also the name of an Enlightenment scientific writer and philosopher."

Didn't hear you sneaking up on me. "Sorry." She handed a small stack of letters over to him. "I've gotten your mail again."

He took the envelopes and pursed his lips. "Amy—"

"Amity."

The weight of his heavy jowls tugged the corners of his mouth into a deep and permanent frown. "Amity. I really must warn you that your holiday decorations are out of compliance with HOA guidelines."

"Really?" she spat. "There's some psychopath in the neighborhood who's gone from a Peeping Tom to attacking women, and you're worried about a few strings of lights?"

"Criminal activity does not fall under the purview of the HOA. As the president—"

"You know what? Your mother gave you the perfect name, because you're soft in the head. There is nothing in the deed restrictions about Christmas lights. I checked, after you sent me that nasty-gram."

"The Architectural Committee—"

"Can shove it. You don't get to arbitrarily make up rules, then selectively enforce them. I'd hate to have to get my attorney involved."

Amity left Fontanelle Bouvier gaping in his driveway like a shutter in a hurricane as she stormed away and slammed the front door.

He has some nerve. My decorations aren't even the most extreme in the neighborhood. Probably just picking on me because he thinks he can get away with it.

She'd used glitter-infused cotton batting to cover up the nest of extension cords that went to all the various outdoor lights—some of them were solar and didn't even need electricity. The twenty-foot inflatable Santa required several guy lines to keep it from blowing around, but they weren't too obtrusive. You could see them, if you *looked*. Maybe the spotlight that shone on the six-foot Grinch, with his sled and antlered dog Max standing next to the chimney, was a *little* over the top, but it was only for a month. The neighbors seemed to like it, anyway—they paused during their dog walks and snapped photos or gathered into clumps on the sidewalk to point at her roof and talk amongst themselves.

Amity had planned to wait until she got settled into the new house for a few months before she got a dog, but between the dangerous prowler and the Home for the Holidays $20 large dog event at the local animal shelter, now seemed like the perfect time. This house was at the end of the cul-de-sac and had a larger-than-average yard, complete with a pristine wood-plank fence. She picked up her car keys.

It was dark when Amity pulled into her garage. Amber and Jax were clipped into the back seats. They had come into the shelter together and may or may not be siblings. The dogs were deeply bonded, and Amity couldn't bring herself to separate them. She had plenty of space, so why not two? They'd keep each other company when she was at work.

Amber, the smaller one, had warm brown eyes, and the pointed ears and thick undercoat of a German Shepherd. Or possibly a husky. She was black with tan highlights on her eyes and muzzle, like a Doberman. She tipped the scales at seventy pounds. Jax was ten pounds heavier and brindle, with some white on his chest and a lot less hair. He also had upright ears, but one eye was ice-blue and the other dark brown.

The dogs seemed unsure of their fates when they'd gotten into Amity's car, and it made her sad. They should be grinning from ear to ear, like the dogs leaving the shelter behind in all those internet videos. Instead, they cowered against the seats, heads down. It took some convincing after she unclipped them to persuade them to get out of the SUV. Once she got them into the house, she dropped their leashes and went back to retrieve the dog food and other supplies from the car.

She found them both hiding under the kitchen table when she returned. Amity set out a bowl of water and two bowls of dry food. Next, she turned on the back porch light and rattled one of the deck chairs against the table to give any critters that might have strayed into her yard a heads-up that they were not alone.

A strip of chicken jerky each was all the incentive they needed to creep out from under the glass table. She took the leashes and led them to the back yard, where she unclipped the leads. The canines spent the next several minutes with their noses to the ground, cataloging all the scents the yard had to offer. Jax started running first. Amber chased him. Then he chased her. It didn't take long for the pups to wear each other out—they'd been in the shelter for six months.

When Amity brought them inside, they were eager for their dinners. While they ate, she set up their crates. The shelter worker had told her they were crate trained and suggested it would be best for everyone if they spent at least the first few nights secured inside while they were getting to know each other.

When Amity went to round the dogs up before she went to bed, she found Jax sitting in the doorway to her darkened bedroom. He tilted his head one way, then the other, as if trying to hone in on something that she could neither hear nor see. Amity snapped on the light, and it appeared to break the spell. She listened carefully to see if there was perhaps a raccoon in the attic, but if there was, it was frozen in fear.

She turned the light off and coaxed Amber and Jax into their crates for the night. They seemed to be more relaxed in their cozy dens than they were outside in the living room. She made sure they each had a toy and went to move her laundry into the dryer. She'd fold it tomorrow.

As she approached her bedroom, she noticed a faint scraping sound. *Is that what Jax had been hearing?* Her pulse quickened, and she swallowed hard. *Is the prowler outside?*

The moment she flipped on the lights, the scratching stopped. Amity hurried across the room and peered out the window. Nothing unusual. Still, after she brushed her teeth, she picked up the metal baseball bat she kept behind her bedroom door and went to sleep on the couch in the living room with Jax and Amber.

On the third morning after bringing Amber and Jax into their forever home, Amity checked the notifications on her phone while she waited for the water in the shower to get hot. One from her neighborhood app already had eighty-nine comments. A woman named Janelle Parker, two streets over, had been attacked by the prowler. She'd tried to shoot him with the handgun she'd recently bought, but he took it away from her and pistol-whipped her severely enough to put her in the hospital.

Tonight's a good night to start leaving the doors to the crates open.

After her shower, she opened her browser to the local paper. The attack had made front page news. Still happened, even with stepped up police patrols in the neighborhood. Fontenelle was organizing a neighborhood watch group. *Maybe he's not completely useless, after all.*

Amity unlocked the doggie door so Jax and Amber could go out into the back yard to take care of business during the day, then went to work.

After she got home, Amity went out for a run and took the dogs with her. She stopped to chat with her catty-corner neighbors, Ken and Maria, who were outside tacking LED icicles to the eaves of their house.

"Oh!" Maria's face brightened. "When did you get dogs? They're beautiful."

When she stepped toward them, Amber moved behind Amity and Jax tucked his tail and let his ears droop. Maria stopped.

"I picked them up from the shelter a few days ago. We're still getting used to each other, but they're more comfortable than they were. This is Jax." Amity raised his leash. "And this is Amber." She indicated the dog behind her.

Ken climbed down from the ladder and looked at the apprehensive canines. "Jax is a spirit dog. He can see this world with his brown eye and the spirit world with his blue eye." He said it so matter-of-factly Amity almost didn't stop to parse it.

She felt the icy hand of dread clutch her insides. *Is that what he'd seen in my bedroom that night? Spirits? Should I call a priest?*

In the daylight, it seemed ridiculous. She shook it off and smiled at the neighbors. "Maybe. Nice talking to you, but I've got to do my running before I run out of gas." Amity waved as she started off at a jog.

There were fliers posted all around the neighborhood for the new watch group, so she pulled off one of the tabs with the website URL and Fontanelle's phone number on it. More and more Christmas decorations were going up, and even though it was 78°, Amity still felt the holiday spirit.

After a shower and a microwaved dinner, she went to the subdivision's website and clicked on the new neighborhood watch page. There was a meeting tomorrow night, so she put that on her calendar and closed the laptop. With a tall glass of ice water in hand, she sat on the couch to watch Netflix. Amber jumped up and settled down with her head in Amity's lap. Jax lay on the floor, his head on her feet.

She fell asleep less than halfway into the movie. When she woke up, Amber was licking her ear.

"Sorry, pups! I didn't skip your dinner on purpose. Come on." Amity hurried to the kitchen, hungry dogs at her heels.

While she was rinsing the cans to put in the recycling, it occurred to her that she hadn't brought the mail in, so she trekked to the end of her driveway to the mailbox.

Junk. Junk. Bill. Amity let out a breath through clenched teeth. She walked next door to read the latest pronouncement from the HOA under the streetlight. They threatened to fine her for her 'noncompliant' Christmas decorations. She tore the letter in half and stuffed it in Fontanelle's mailbox.

Now that her adrenalin was up, she was nowhere near being able to sleep. She scoured the web for ways to deal with troublesome HOAs until well past her bedtime. Amity brushed her teeth and slipped into bed. Amber hopped up onto the mattress and curled up next to Amity's feet.

A low growl woke Amity from a deep sleep. It was the type of growl that she felt in her chest just as much as heard. Both dogs stood on the bed, facing her. Jax growled again.

Fear chilled Amity's skin and dripped down her spine like ice water. *Was this why they'd been dumped at the shelter? They'd turned on their master?*

Don't show fear. Don't show fear. Don't show fear. "Easy, there, guys. Can we talk about this?"

Amber snarled and barked.

Jax leaped.

Not at Amity, but at the window behind her bed. It was then she saw a figure in a hoodie fleeing. The dogs bounded out of the room, and seconds later, she heard the flap, flap noise of them exiting the doggie door. She grabbed her phone and dialed 911, speaking with the operator as she hurried out the front door to the sound of barking and snarling. The prowler must have left the gate open as he ran.

She almost laughed. In his flight from the dogs, he had apparently tripped over the guy lines that held the noncompliant twenty-foot Santa in place. Jax stood on his chest, growling, and Amber barked in his face. Amity didn't even try to call off the dogs until the first police car arrived minutes later. If he got bitten, well, he shouldn't have been sneaking around her property. Amity was grateful the puppers came right to her, and she didn't have to try to tug them away.

The officers handcuffed the prowler and helped him to his feet. The hood fell back and Amity blinked rapidly, not believing what she saw.

Fontanelle Bouvier glared at her from police custody.

It Came Upon a Midnight Clear
By A.B. Richards

MONICA Ridley gasped. "That's—that's a real baby!"

She gathered the squirming infant into her arms. "Who are you? Are you okay?"

"You know babies don't talk, right?" Cecelia Camp, Monica's best friend, cocked her head.

"Yes, I know." She rocked her body back and forth. "We should call the police or something. Maybe take this little guy to the hospital?"

Cecelia bent to pick up the doll that should have been lying in the manger. "How do you know it's a guy?" She dropped the carved baby Jesus into the wooden box, then glanced at the life-sized statue of the Virgin Mary as the clunk of its head striking the box boomed around the nativity scene.

"Girl or boy, we can't just stand here all night. This baby needs help."

"I'll call 911." Cecelia pulled out her phone.

It took less than ten minutes for the police and ambulance to show up.

After handing over the child to paramedics and giving the police a statement, Monica and Cecelia continued on their way to the Christmas party.

Three days later, Monica got a call from the office of a judge in the family courts, asking her to come testify at a hearing. They only gave her two days' notice, and her supervisor was reluctant to let her take the day off. But a printed copy of the subpoena made the case.

Monica wasn't sure what to expect. She met an attorney in the judge's chambers and gave her statement about finding the baby.

The judge nodded along the whole time Monica spoke. When she finished, the jurist straightened some papers on her desk. "Ms. Ridley, do you have children?"

"Yes, but they're both grown. One's away at college. The other lives in Philadelphia."

"Do you still have any baby clothes, playpen, baby paraphernalia?"

"Maybe a few things. Why do you ask?"

The judge slid her glasses down her nose a little way. "As you may or may not be aware, the child protective services system is facing a critical shortage of foster parents. Would you be willing to look after him until his family can be located, or an infant placement becomes available in the system, whichever comes first?"

Monica blinked rapidly. "I-I don't know what to say."

"There is compensation available, Ms. Ridley."

"It's not about the money. A baby, well, a baby is a lot of work. And my job…"

"It's okay, Ms. Ridley. You don't have to take him. We've been calling him Sam, by the way. He's too young to understand anything about Christmas, and the nurses will be available to take care of him at the hospital."

Monica swallowed. Christmas at the hospital seemed like a forlorn prospect, even if Sam was too young to be aware of it. "You know, I'm off work next week. I suppose I could take him. For the holidays, anyway. Maybe he's been stolen, and his parents are desperately looking for him. It shouldn't take too long to find them, not if they're searching, right?"

"Mrs. Ridley, I can't guarantee that's the case. And you would need to arrange daycare if he's still in your custody when you need to return to work."

"Of course." Then she smiled. "It'll surprise the heck out of my family, me turning up with a baby." *Maybe Suzanne will get baby fever and produce that grandchild I've been waiting for...*

❊ ❊ ❊

Monica woke up to blue and red strobes flashing in her window. She glanced at the crib next to her bed to see Sam peacefully asleep before she got up and peered through the glass.

Seven police cars, lights flashing, were parked on both sides of the road, so she couldn't tell if they were at her next-door neighbors or the neighbors across the street. A Crime Scene Unit van pulled up and two people got out. One went to the door of the next-door neighbor and the other opened the back of the vehicle.

Sam coughed, and Monica drew the curtains. He was stirring, so she picked him up and changed him before going downstairs. The pediatrician at the hospital estimated him to be about three months old, so he wasn't yet mobile. Still young enough to stay where he was put, but that wouldn't last much longer.

She left him in a bouncy chair, playing with the attached toys, while she mixed the formula. She smiled as he cooed and giggled in the living room.

When she returned to the baby, she set the milk on an end table by the couch and scooped Sam up. At first, he took the bottle, but then spat out the nipple, turning his head away when she tried to poke it back into his mouth. She raised him to her shoulder and burped him, then tried feeding him again with the same result.

Monica frowned at the bottle—he'd drunk less than an ounce when he had typically been drinking four or five. He didn't seem to be in any distress, so she put the bottle in the fridge, determined to try again later.

"Time for a morning walk, Sammie." Monica put a sweater on the baby and buckled him into the stroller.

It was the perfect pretext for snooping at what was happening next door.

A clump of people stood in front of Monica's house. She waved to Oliver, who lived two doors down.

"Hey." Monica glanced over her shoulder. "What's going on at the Walton's house?"

"Flora's missing."

"What?" Monica pushed the stroller back and forth to keep Sam from fussing.

"Yeah. Walter says he got up this morning, and she wasn't in bed. There was a little blood on the floor in the kitchen, but nothing else was out of place."

"Were the doors locked?"

"I guess. Don't really know."

"You know she's been diagnosed with dementia."

Oliver rubbed his jaw. "But most days, she's fine."

"Well then, how does Walter know she didn't go to the grocery store or something?"

"Haven't talked to him. But their car's in the driveway."

Monica adjusted the stroller's sunshade. "She may have wandered off. I'm sure she'll be located, safe and sound. I'll keep my eyes out for her while we're out."

"Good idea. Have a nice walk."

Monica didn't see Flora Walton on her walk that day. Or the next. Sam had started guzzling formula again, so she noted his brief refusal in her notebook, under 'Questions to Ask Pedi' for the next doctor visit.

Morgan Simpson from across the street disappeared next. The next day, both Salvador and Theresa Menendez, three doors down, vanished.

"Mom?"

"Monica? You sound… strange. Are you okay?"

"Yeah. I know we weren't supposed to come until Christmas Eve, but can Sam and I come a day early? And maybe stay over a while?"

"Of course. But what's wrong?"

"People have been disappearing in the neighborhood. I'm scared, Mom."

"I'll get your room ready. Your dad can put the bassinet in there for you."

"Thanks, Mom. I've got a doctor appointment for Sam, so we'll come straight from there."

"You be careful. See you later, sweetie."

"Good morning, Ms. Ripley. What seems to be going on with Sam?"

"Well, Dr. Nguyen, he just seems to sleep more than usual. Some days he eats, some days he doesn't. He looks fine, but I just feel like something's wrong."

"He's gained almost two pounds. You remember when babies are growing, they sleep a lot. He could also be teething. Their little gums get itchy and sore before the teeth erupt. There's a new oral anesthetic out—I'll give you some samples and maybe that will help."

"Thanks."

Dr. Nguyen examined Sam but didn't find anything noteworthy. "He looks great. Very healthy. If he's still being finicky about eating after the holidays, bring him back in. I think it's just teething, and it will pass soon."

"Isn't he a little young to be teething?"

"It's earlier than average, but I've seen them start even younger. I attended a baby at the hospital last month that was born with four teeth."

"Alright. You have a great holiday, Dr. Nguyen."

"You too, Ms. Ridley."

Monica's mother, Ruby, sat in the armchair and held a sleeping Sam.

Nash wiped sweat from his forehead. "You'd never know it was anywhere near Christmas. Gotta be 85°."

"I know, Daddy. Not that we ever have a white Christmas, but there's supposed to be a cold front on the way."

"Can't come soon enough. Need a good freeze to cut down on fleas and mosquitos." He reached out to scratch one of the two oversized black cats that had tucked themselves into loaves next to him on the sofa. Glimmer had a small white streak on his throat and golden eyes, while Spartacus had green eyes and a seemingly Vantablack coat.

Both cats stared at Ruby. "I don't think either of them has ever seen a baby before."

"Probably right about that," Nash said.

Monica tried to stifle a yawn, but it got away from her.

"You must be exhausted, sweetie. Let me put Sam in the bassinet so you can go to bed." Her mother carefully rose out of the chair.

"Thanks, Mom."

The baby was stowed and Monica brushed her teeth. She fell into bed like a marionette whose strings were suddenly cut. The adrenalin had dissipated from her system, and exhaustion took its place.

The sound of cats growling briefly woke her, but she settled back into sleep within seconds. By the time Sam began to cry, streaks of sunlight poked through the curtains. She changed him and took him into the kitchen to mix a bottle. Monica kicked the cat food dish and sent it spinning across the floor. Spartacus pinned his ears at her, and Glimmer hissed.

"It was an accident, guys. Sorry."

She took Sam into the living room, where he drank the entire bottle, so she mixed a second. He drank most of that one, too.

"Looks like his appetite is coming back," Ruby said.

"Where's Dad?"

"Airport run."

"Better get dressed, then."

Ruby watched Sam while Monica showered. As she leaned over her suitcase, holding the towel that wrapped her wet hair in one hand, Monica noticed a wiry black hair on the floor. She picked it up. It was thick and about three inches long. Frowning, she set it on the dresser while she put on her clothes.

Monica carried the weird hair with her when she returned to the living room. "Mom? Have you had Bigfoot as a houseguest?" She held up her find.

Ruby scowled at it for a moment. "Your Uncle Tim shot a feral hog and had it taxidermied. Brought it around to show your father. Probably fell off of that nightmare."

"He's not bringing it around for Christmas, is he?"

"Lord, I hope not."

Uncle Tim left the stuffed hog's head at home when he came for Christmas lunch. Monica was delighted to see how much her daughter's husband, Kenny, played with Sam. It was a wonderful, exhausting holiday. By Sunday afternoon, everyone except Monica and Sam had left.

Ruby handed Monica a fresh bottle of formula. "What are you going to do, sweetie?"

"I hadn't scheduled time off next week. They're expecting me at work tomorrow."

"Do you have childcare arrangements made?"

"I didn't have a lot of time to look, but the few places I called had no vacancies until summer."

"And you haven't heard anything from the courts?"

"Not a word."

Ruby sat on the other end of the sofa from Monica. "Would you like your father and I to come stay for a little bit, while you're trying to get everything wiggled into place? We'd have to bring the boys."

Monica wanted to jump up and dance around. But Sam was having a meal. "Sure, Mom. If it's convenient for you."

"I'd feel better if you weren't alone in your house after what's been going on in your neighborhood. And you need the childcare."

Thursday night rolled around quicker than Monica had expected. The office was dead, nearly half the staff out on vacation, and no clients breathing down their necks. She went home on time every day.

Nash blotted his lips on the napkin and set his fork down on the dinner plate. "Your rosebush really needs cutting back. Do you have a pruner?"

"I think there's one in the shed."

There was a small wooden structure where her ex-husband had kept all of the gardening equipment. She used a lawn service now, and hadn't opened the door on that place in years.

"I'll take a look in the morning."

After Monica bathed and fed Sam, then rocked him to sleep, she crept into her own bed. It was luxurious to stretch out and lie in the center of the mattress. She was asleep as soon as she got still.

The yowling of angry cats woke her. Disoriented from having been jolted out of a deep sleep, Monica rubbed her eyes. The caterwauling came again. Monica swung her feet over the side of the bed.

And she felt her heart stop.

Sam wasn't in his crib.

Monica ran down the hall, toward the furious felines, hitting every light switch on the way. "Sam! Sam, where are you?"

He wasn't even strong enough to sit up, much less climb out of his bed. Cold dread flooded over her. Maybe the neighborhood killer hadn't left the area, after all.

The cats were in the kitchen. As she got closer, she could hear clicking and scratching. Was someone trying to climb out the window with Sam? She heard a door open behind her, and assumed it was her parents. "Sam's missing!"

The cats hissed.

Monica snapped on the light. A scream died in her throat with a strangled choke.

This was a dream. A nightmare. Nothing like this existed in real life.

Glimmer and Spartacus stood on the kitchen table, ears pinned, teeth bared, and fur fluffed out to terrifying proportions. The back door was partway open, and light from the motion-activated back porch floods fell on something Monica couldn't comprehend.

It was a spider. The top joint of its legs was well above the countertop, perhaps four feet high. Wiry black hairs covered its pallid body and its bloated abdomen gave off a putrid luminescence, a pale green glow that seemed oily with decay.

She expected eight malevolent eyes to regard her as its swollen head turned in her direction. What she saw was much worse.

This impossible spider had a human face. Mostly. Instead of a lower jaw, thick, hairy spider's fangs opened and closed, the mandibles glistening with venom and menace.

Somewhere over Monica's left shoulder, Ruby screamed.

The spider pushed the door the rest of the way open and fled into the yard. It shimmied up a tree and disappeared into the darkness.

Monica collapsed to her knees and vomited. Nash called 911 and within minutes the place was swarming with police. Crime scene technicians prowled through the house. Detectives questioned Monica, Ruby, and Nash separately. Monica described the male face that she saw but couldn't bring herself to tell Detective Findlay that it had been attached to a giant spider.

Shouting arose from the backyard. The officers who had been searching out there came running to the back door. Monica noticed the shed door stood open, and her insides clenched.

She jumped up and ran out of the kitchen to the shed. "Sam! Sam!"

A cop tried to stop her from looking inside that open door, but she twisted out of his grasp.

She wished she'd let him catch her.

The interior light shone on garden tools, plastic flowerpots, and a pile of bodies. Mummified bodies. As if every drop of moisture had been extracted from them. It was impossible to identify the shriveled features of the deceased. But Monica recognized Flora Wharton's pink sweater. Morgan Simpson's crocheted hat. Theresa Menendez' embroidered dress. Salvador Menendez's shockingly thick moustache.

All of the desiccated bodies of the missing were there.

All of them, except for Sam's.

Dreaming of a White Christmas

By Artemis Greenleaf

REGENT Hawley coughed into a tissue and sighed at the spatter of blood. It was getting worse. *Damned holiday travel.*

He was late. His original flight had been canceled due to weather conditions, as had the two planes he'd been on standby for. He had to see his brother. If he didn't get there by tomorrow...

Regent was dying. He knew that. But he had to make it home to see his brother. Something terrible would happen if he didn't, he was sure of it.

He slouched in the hard plastic chair and stared at a giant artificial evergreen wreath that hung behind the gate agent's desk. He wondered if the shiny red ornaments were intended to represent holly berries or if they were just part of the red and gold holiday theme that pervaded the airport. He pulled his green jacket closer around his shoulders.

The soft-edged darkness of the second longest night of the year had converted the terminal windows into mirrors, and Regent surveyed the dim terminal obliquely. Some delayed travelers had found hotel rooms. The remainder slumped in chairs or lay on the floor, using their luggage as pillows. It made Regent think of the aftermath of some great battle, with bodies strewn hither and yon. Dark circles shadowed his own eyes, peering out of the glass at him from above a bushy grey beard.

He coughed again and went to the men's room. He needed more paper towels.

When he returned, two gate agents had arrived at the desk. Regent wanted to make sure he was first on the standby list, so he bee-lined his way to them.

"Ma'am? Excuse me. Is flight 197 going to depart tonight?"

"The plane's on its way. Two hours behind schedule, but it should arrive soon. Right now, it looks like 197 will be able to get underway, but the weather's pretty dicey, so I can't promise." The agent paused to give him a once-over. "Are you feeling all right? You look a little peaked."

More piqued than peaked. "I've been in this airport for 36 hours. I'm tired and desperate for a hot shower. I also have urgent business at home. Of course, I'm not feeling all right."

His agitation brought on another coughing fit, and he barely got the paper towel to his mouth in time.

The agent nodded sympathetically. "I'll check you in for stand-by."

"Thank you."

His text chime went off on the way back to his uncomfortable chair. "How was your flight? XD"

"Glad my travel misery amuses someone, Calli."

"LOL. So much snow. All the airports will be closed."

"Are you doing this?"

"You're the one who left. I have come to like it this way."

"Meh. Seasons change."

"Not if you don't see your brother tomorrow."

"Wut"

"You know the rules. If he doesn't spill your blood, he doesn't get your power."

Regent yawned. His chest felt like a mastodon was standing on it and it hurt to breathe. "It's just a formality. Has been for a long time," he bluffed.

"LOL. I, however, have spilled your blood. How is your cough?"

"?????"

"The shortbread I made you for your trip? It was spelled. Wanted it to look like a sickness to keep you off the plane, if it managed to get around the snow I sent. The one who spills your blood on the winter solstice gets your power. Usually been your brother. But this year, it's me."

"And when Brigid comes in the spring?"

"If the Oak King fails to take your power, it stops the wheel, and spring will not come."

"Why, Calli?"

"The Earth has a fever. She must be cooled."

"People will starve in a year-long winter."

"More will starve in the heat."

"You can't do this. Not again."

"LOL. Guess again, Holly King. As ruler of the waning year, you of all people should embrace the dark and cold."

"Do you really think a year without spring or summer will make a difference?"

"A year? A thousand, or a million. Whatever it takes. As you well know, I've done it before."

Wooly mammoths and saber-tooth cats tramped across the tundra in his mind's eye. Activity at the kiosk drew his gaze. A plane was taxiing into the gate. *So far, so good. Please let me be on it when it takes off.*

When Regent opened his eyes, he was not in the airport. Nor on a plane. He was in a hospital bed and a nurse, facing away from him, was adjusting the drip on his IV fluids. He tried to talk, but there was an oxygen mask covering his face.

The nurse turned around and smiled at him.

Regent winced as he bent his elbow and moved the IV catheters around, but he clawed the plastic covering away from his mouth. "Calli! What—"

She raised a finger to her lips. "Don't try to talk."

He tried to sit up and began to cough. Bright blood spattered on the blue blanket. Calli ran a finger across the spot and rotated her wrist to look at it. She gave a half smile to the red stain on her hand. "Today is the solstice. Your power is mine, Holly King, and I stop the wheel, the turning of the seasons. Sleep. Your time will come again."

He could feel his life force draining away. His vision got narrower and narrower, then greyed out.

❄ ❄ ❄

Regent gradually became aware of warmth on his cheeks. The Holly King sucked in a deep breath, bringing with it the rich smell of moist earth and the fragile scent of crocus blooms. His eyelids fluttered open, and he found himself lying on his side in a forest clearing. Pockmarked melting snow had retreated to the deepest shade.

He sat up and found the Cailleach grinning at him.

"Nice nap?"

He shook his head to clear the cobwebs. "Nap? How long?"

"It's been a while." She nodded.

"Decades?" He looked down at his muscular arms and scratched his beardless chin.

"Centuries. But the balance has been restored, and the wheel restarted."

She led him through the trees to a small meadow. Two silver capsules, perhaps the size of picnic tables, floated above the grass. They settled to the ground and three people emerged from one and four from the other.

"I told you!" A woman jogged toward the treeline, but not directly toward them. "I told you the snow was melting."

The people held up silver devices, as if they were recording the snow accumulation. Their excited voices faded into the trees as they continued exploring.

Calli pointed toward the horizon in the valley below. In the distance, Regent could just make out what appeared to be an area where immense blisters had erupted from the skin of the earth.

"They had to build domes over their cities, and a lot of farms to survive. Run on hydrogen and sunlight. It isn't perfect, but works well enough."

The ground started to shake, and Regent grabbed for a tree trunk to steady himself. "The Earth heaves. Will it divide itself again?"

"Look over there."

A herd of wooly mammoths trotted out of the trees into the meadow, each six-ton step sending shockwaves through the soil. At last, they stopped and began stuffing grass into their mouths with their hairy trunks.

"I don't understand. They died out such a long time ago."

"They've been brought back. Somebody thought they'd help cool down the planet by mowing down trees to create grasslands, which reflect more heat than forests."

"Did it work?"

Calli shrugged. "Hard to say. I was dumping so much snow everywhere. Maybe, maybe not. But there are a lot of them around now. They may have to resurrect dire wolves and cave hyenas to balance out the population."

"Huh."

Calli pulled a silver dagger from her belt and cut the back of her hand. She dabbed some of the resulting blood on his forehead between his eyes. "Your power, returned."

She fell to the ground in a heap. He knelt beside her. Her face changed from crone to maid, and Brigid, the goddess of the light half of the year, opened her eyes.

"Where am I? What's happened?"

He extended his hand. "Come on. I've got a lot to tell you."

Regent was present at the autumnal equinox, when the dark half of the year started and the Cailleach's reign began. He was middle-aged now, and he was looking forward to his six-month nap.

Calli would be with him at the winter solstice, when his brother, the Oak King, would spill his blood and rule the waxing half of the year. He had some stories to share, that was for sure. The time was approaching, and the Holly King spent some time wandering among the people.

Inside the city, the ceiling of the dome was covered with some material, or perhaps tiny screens, which mirrored the sky outside. Evergreen wreaths appeared on doors. Colorful lights wrapped around posts and railings. An animated comet traveled across the artificial sky. Regent was an old man now, and his back hurt most of the time. He stroked his long white beard and adjusted the pack on his shoulders.

A boy of about six paused to look at Regent, his eyes getting big. "Is it really you? Are you...?"

Regent laughed, the large dinner he'd just eaten distending his belly. He slung the bag off his shoulder and reached inside, pulling out a package. With his left index finger to his lips, he tossed the parcel to the child.

So stunned was the boy that he didn't even attempt to catch it. The package glanced off his shoulder and he bent to retrieve it.

"Kris! Hurry up!" a woman called.

"Thank you!" The boy stashed the prize in his jacket, turned, and ran to his mother.

Regent left the dome and walked to the forest. A wren flitted out of a snow-laden pine and perched on his shoulder. Heavy footsteps shook the trees and rattled the snow from the branches. Regent smiled at the massive creature that approached him.

"Well, well, well. It's been a very long time since I've seen your kind. You must be another project of the resurrectionists."

The Irish Elk stopped in front of Regent. He stood seven feet tall at the shoulder, and his great antlers easily spanned twelve feet. The Holly King led the elk to a large rock—Regent's days of springing lightly up were well past—and he clambered onto the hulking beast's back. The tiny bird settled again on his shoulder as the enormous deer carried them through the snowy forest.

Regent was glad his brother would meet him soon.

He had so much to tell him.

A Christmas Coyote

By A.B. Richards

DALE Wayne McGill grumbled to himself as he pulled the blackout curtains closed against his neighbors' blinking holiday lights.

"I hope that life-sized Santa in his sleigh falls off the roof and shatters into a million pieces. It'd be good riddance," he muttered at the house across the street.

At least tonight was Christmas Eve, and all this foolishness would be over soon.

He plunked down in his recliner and pulled his laptop over onto his legs. Dale doom-scrolled on social media for a little while, until the harsh beep of a new notification on his neighborhood app interrupted him. A yawn broke through his clenched jaws as he tapped the screen.

Bah! The house at the end of the block had won the decoration contest. That didn't surprise him. He frowned at the picture of the gaudy lights and big box store decorations. Their ridiculous lights and cheesy scene of penguins and polar bears having a Christmas party, complete with tree, gifts, and a fish buffet had drawn visitors from all over the city and snarled traffic in the neighborhood for weeks.

To add insult to injury, they were too stupid to know that penguins live in the southern hemisphere and polar bears in the north, and would never, ever meet in the natural world. He couldn't wait for them to take that mess down.

In another post, somebody was hoping for gas money donations to go see their mother in Lubbock. She'd punctuated her message with a tacky, over-bright GIF of a jack-in-the-box springing out and spreading its hands to reveal the words 'Merry Christmas!'

You're too poor to buy gas, what do you have to be merry about?

Further down the page, some idiot wondered why their grass had gone brown. In December. Dale rolled his eyes and yawned again.

His eyelids drooped, but he continued reading. Ah, there it was. The inevitable PRC post.

Possibly Rabid Coyote spotted this morning! Don't let your kids out alone—it's too dangerous!!!!!!!!!! When will the HOA fix this?!!?!

The text was below a blurry photo of something that could have been a German shepherd lurking in winter-bare shrubbery.

Dale scrolled through the predictable comments. Roadrunner jokes. Coyote deniers. Coyote defenders. Warnings to keep pets indoors.

He'd rest his eyes for a minute before he continued.

A scratching on the back door startled Dale awake.

Probably some lost dog. You're at the wrong place, buddy. He set the laptop aside and got up to investigate.

Frosty air—not freezing, but uncomfortably cold—swirled around him as he stepped out onto the icy concrete slab.

A coyote sat on his covered patio. Its mouth was bloody, and one front leg hung at a disturbing angle.

Dale waved his arms. "Shoo! Get outta here!"

The song dog remained in place and fixed him with its yellow eyes. "Have you forgotten me so soon, Dale?"

The man's jaw dropped open. *Am I having a stroke?* "C-c-coyotes don't talk."

The canine's lips pulled back into a broken-toothed smile. "Seven days ago, Dale. You hit me with your car and left me to die. My mate is still looking for me."

"It's your own fault. You should have had enough sense to stay out of the road. You were probably rabid, anyways. Did you a favor."

The coyote flicked an ear. "Is it always the victim's fault?"

"Pretty much. People put themselves in bad situations, then whine about how unfair everything is."

A yip-yip-yipping that sounded a lot like laughter came from the canine.

"Remember you said that, Dale Wayne McGill."

The song dog turned and limped to the tall back fence, then bounded up to the top and dropped down on the other side.

Dale shivered and then belched, sticking his tongue out at the sour taste that came with it. Maybe he'd left that carton of eggnog sitting on the counter a little too long, after all.

He turned to go back inside the warm house, but the door had locked behind him. He swore at the knob, but it refused to turn. In frustration, he kicked the door, but that only hurt his ankle. There was a key in the front under a potted plant, but the side gate was latched in the front, with no way to open it from this side. Dale groaned.

Rustling from a centrally placed flowerbed made him spin around, expecting to see the trippy coyote again.

The iceberg rosebush moved, but he couldn't tell why. Wasn't the wind, because all the other plants were still. He stalked toward the quaking shrub as the browning petals of spent flowers drifted to the ground like fat, dirty snowflakes.

As he approached, the bush stopped moving. A low and chunky shadow slipped out of the dying border plants. Two white stripes started at the crown of its head and ran all the way to its bushy tail.

The skunk stamped its feet and raised itself into a handstand, turning its butt to Dale and waving it's fluffed tail.

"Easy there. You just go on about your business. You already been rootin' around in my garden diggin' stuff up. You got your grubs, now just get outta here. I'm tired of you varmints tearin' up my yard."

The animal continued its display, and Dale wondered if he had any hydrogen peroxide. It seemed like yesterday, as he remembered the time Charlotte let the dog out in the backyard and he'd run straight into a skunk. Dale and Charlotte hadn't been married long, just moved into the house earlier that week.

The rose bed wasn't there then.

Nothing was there, except a huge burr oak tree in the back corner.

Dale had made a desperate run to the 24-hour grocery for peroxide. They already had baking soda and detergent. He'd thought a Labrador retriever would love the water, but Pepper hated baths with a passion, and it had taken both him and Charlotte to wrestle the dog into the tub. They had been laughing so hard at his pitiful complaints that the soapy dog was able to slip out of the tub and lead them on a merry chase around the house. By the time they'd captured and rinsed him, they were both wet to the skin. Soggy clothes had to come off, and they'd made love. The memory of the warmth of her body as she lay in his arms chased away the chill for a moment.

Then Charlotte had ruined everything. She went and got herself pregnant. How many times had he told her he wasn't ready for kids?

It had shattered him when she went away. He put the iceberg rose there to remind him of her frozen heart—she didn't care about him at all, just used him as a sperm donor and expected him to be happy about it.

While Dale was lost in reverie, the skunk shuffled away.

The chittering trill of a raccoon caught his attention. The trash panda was raiding his winter vegetable garden. The snow peas Dale had planted in October were just starting to produce and the greedy bandit was gnawing on the tender pods.

He charged the animal, waving his arms. "Shoo! Git!"

The raccoon rose to its hind legs, a delicate pea pod with a few petals of the white flower still attached sticking out of its mouth.

"Quit eating all my food!" he shouted.

The raccoon resumed chewing.

"I'll fix you, just you wait and see."

Dale stormed back to his house, completely forgetting his predicament. *That fat raccoon won't eat lead tonight. But next time…*

He stood at the edge of the patio and glared at the creature. He didn't want to touch it. If it wasn't scared of him, it could very well have rabies.

How long do raccoons live, anyway? Nah, couldn't be…

Every stray or injured thing in the neighborhood had found its way to their door after Katie and Neil had moved into his house. They had been fifteen and seventeen. He hadn't really wanted them, but his sister and her husband had died in a boating accident, and the kids had no other place to go. Katie fed the feral cats, even though he told her not to. Damn things pissed everywhere.

She bought a concrete bird bath and put the bowl on the ground under the oak tree for the wildlife. He had dumped it out almost every day. He didn't want a mosquito farm. Never caught her refilling it, but she must have, because it was always full.

And then there was the baby raccoon. The wretched mother had nested in his attic, and he'd trapped her, along with her filthy brood, and driven them far out into the country. But he'd missed one, and its frantic trilling for its mother had kept him awake that night. He'd bought some rat poison on the way home from work to get rid of it.

But by the time he'd arrived, the kids had caught it, and Katie already had a wildlife rescuer lined up to come get it in the morning. They'd told her how to care for it until then. Dale had to admit that the thing was too stinkin' cute, curled on Katie's shoulder and nestling in her hair.

Maybe it didn't eat much, but it was still an extra mouth to feed, and he already had two too many of those. At least Neil would graduate at the end of the month, and thanks to their parents' generous insurance payout and money from their estate, go off to college. Dale had made plans for that money, but it had gone into trusts for each of the children, and he couldn't touch it. His sister had left him only a pittance for their care. Which would shrink after Neil left. He was still stuck with Katie for another two years. Another two years of her eating his food, using his electricity, and taking up space in his house.

When he'd told Neil that she'd run away, his nephew was not the least bit surprised. But he was angry—even had the nerve to blame Dale for chasing her off.

So Dale planted vegetables. The bed was little less than six feet long and probably would never make up for all the food they'd taken from him, but at least it was something. A middle finger to the tribulations fortune had thrown at him.

Hissing to his left made him look. A 'possum had waddled into the yard and noticed the raccoon, which continued its pea feast and ignored the alarmed marsupial.

"Why are you here? There hasn't been cat food out in years."

Unlike the coyote, the 'possum didn't reply. It carefully made its way to the new flowerbed and started sniffing around the pile of fresh dirt. Dale rubbed his lower back and snorted. He wished Neil had been able to help him with digging that bed. He was older now, and yardwork wasn't as easy as it used to be.

Dale saw Neil exactly once every year, on Christmas Eve, when his nephew, at the insistence of his wife, grudgingly came around to invite him to Christmas lunch. Knowing, he was about as welcome as a raging case of syphilis, Dale flatly refused the invitation. Every. Year. Dale wished Neil's wife would just give up already. It wasn't happening, and this fool's errand probably irritated Neil as much as it did him.

This year was different, though. Neil and his wife had had a baby. They'd named her Katherine, after his missing sister. He'd never given up hope that she'd come home one day, even after all these years. Dale had called him a sucker and said that Katie had probably OD'd in an alley somewhere a long time ago.

They'd fought. Neil would never darken his door again after this.

And now, after a worse-than-usual Christmas Eve, here he was, stuck in his backyard at three in the morning.

Figures.

Dale weighed his options. He could cover himself with the chase lounge cushions and try to sleep. Maybe he'd be able to flag down some neighbors in the daylight.

No. They'd all be indoors opening presents. Nobody'd be outside until at least lunchtime.

He could break a window. But then he'd have a broken window that would let cold air in for the rest of the night and would cost money to repair.

As he saw it, the only choice he had was to climb over the fence into his north neighbor's backyard. She never locked her gate, so he could let himself out and retrieve the key to go in through his front door.

Dale dragged one of the deck chairs over to the fence and propped it against the wood, so it didn't topple over when he climbed on it. Placing a foot on each armrest, he was now tall enough to peer over into the neighbor's yard. As he stood there, calculating the best way to get his leg over the wooden planks, a coyote howled.

And then another, and another, and another. It sounded like there was a whole pack of them in the yard below. Dale couldn't see them, but they had to be there somewhere. He could feel the high-pitched yipping and wailing deep in his body. The eerie wall of sound got louder and louder, until he let go of the fence and covered his ears with his hands, trying to block out the noise.

Dale stumbled off the chair and ran across the yard to get as far away from the animals as he could. He tripped and fell, sprawling into the shallow excavation of the new flowerbed.

❊ ❊ ❊

The thin winter sunlight of Christmas day washed over Dale Wayne McGill as he stood at the center of his backyard. The uprooted iceberg rose lay on its side, next to a pile of dirt. Two men carefully removed Charlotte's skeletal remains from the pit and placed her bones on a blue tarp.

To his right, a crew of men dug up his vegetable garden. They had trampled his Sicilian kale into the ground.

Nobody has any respect for other people's property these days.

The cuffs chaffed his wrists, but at least his hands were in front of his body. His back and shoulders were sore from digging up that new bed yesterday. Too bad he'd run out of lime and couldn't finish it then. And of course, the stores were going to be closed on Christmas day.

Why do these things always happen to me? If Neil had just left me alone…

A man in a polo shirt and khakis walked up to the police officer standing next to Dale. "I got some cockamamie story about rabid coyotes from the neighbor. Who found the body?"

"Mr. McGill locked himself out of the house last night. Lady next door heard howling and went to check it out. That's when she saw someone trying to climb over the fence into her yard—didn't realize it was her neighbor. She called 911, and when we got here, we found him unconscious in the backyard, with his nephew's body, in that new flowerbed. He got real mad and started shouting about his wife and niece, and asking why we didn't just dig them up, too, while we were destroying his garden."

"Why's he still here?"

"You see that big flowerbed that runs along the back fence?"

Dale clenched his teeth.

Damn PRC.

Oh, Tannenbaum

By Artemis Greenleaf

WHAT about this one?" Carolyn asked.

Clark regarded the tree next to his wife. "I don't think so. Look up. It's really lopsided."

She laughed. "That side could go against the wall."

"Then I'd have to set an anchor bolt into the sheetrock, so it didn't tip over when the ornaments go on."

"You know I was joking, right?"

Something rustled in the leaves in the underbrush to their left. Both of their heads swiveled toward the sound.

Carolyn craned her head around. "Can you tell what it is?"

He shook his head. "Smaller than a deer, though. Probably a raccoon or a 'possum. Nothin' to worry about."

She started back toward the trail. "We should make a decision. Won't be long before dark."

"Let's go just a little bit further."

Carolyn scanned the woods around them and pulled her jacket tighter. "Okay. But not too much further."

Clark took her hand and led her deeper into the forest. Another rustling in the bushes made Carolyn stop. The animal seemed to be moving away from them at a good clip.

"I don't like this, Clark. Maybe we should just come back in the morning."

"We aren't going to have time to mess with the Christmas tree tomorrow. We've got too much to do before we go to the Dempsey's party."

She sighed. "You're right. It probably *is* a raccoon or something. I'm feelin' a little spooked, that's all. Just my imagination running wild."

He squeezed her hand. "It will be dark soon, so we should get a move on. Don't want to run up on some feral hogs or a cougar."

They resumed their hike at an accelerated pace. Carolyn studied the trees on the left of the path and Clark looked at the ones on the right.

She tugged his hand. "What about this one?"

They walked over to it for a closer look. The evergreen was mostly conical, with an odd branch sticking out here and another there. The ten-foot tree would go perfectly in their two-story tall great room, next to the fireplace.

Clark set his backpack on the ground. "Let's do it."

He pulled out work gloves and an electric chain saw, then cut the tree down, severing it as close to ground level as possible. Clark returned the saw to his pack and dragged the tree's corpse down the trail to the waiting four-wheeler. By the time they had secured it to the vehicle with bungees, darkness had seeped down from the bare branches of the slumbering trees.

Carolyn climbed into the passenger seat and crossed her arms—the temperature was falling fast now that the winter sun had slunk below the horizon. Clark cranked up the ATV and three sets of headlights cut through the gloom like bear claws through a honeycomb.

She wished he'd go faster, but knew better than to say anything that might be taken as a criticism of his driving. The house would be warm and bright, and they'd be safe from the malevolent eyes that Carolyn had felt as they'd trekked through the deepest woods.

Clark dropped the tree at the front door—he'd drive the four-wheeler back to the barn later. Their two sausage dogs, Brat and Knock, barked when the door opened, tails wagging. As soon as he started dragging the tree through the door, their wagging tails tucked between their legs and they trotted off to hide under the sofa in the den.

He paused. "What's got into them? Not like they haven't seen a Christmas tree before.'

Carolyn closed the door behind her husband and the conifer. "When we lived in the city, our trees were less than half this size. There's probably all kinds of smells from the forest on this one. Maybe a coyote marked his territory or something. I'm sure they'll be out for a good sniff soon."

Clark resumed dragging the tree into the great room. Carolyn helped get it into the stand and level it. Once it was in place, he pushed a lever with his foot that tightened metal claws around the tree trunk. When he was sure it was stable, she poured the water she'd mixed with tree preservative earlier into the stand. He put the lights on the tree while she made hot cocoa.

Isobel, the feral tabby kitten that had turned up at their door a few weeks ago, galloped on white-tipped paws into the great room. She took one look at the unexpected tree and bolted.

"What's with her?" Clark plugged in another string of lights.

"Kitten zoomies, I guess. You know how she is."

Carolyn sat on the couch and dipped a chocolate chip biscotti into her cocoa. "Lookin' good!"

Clark grinned. He was almost done stringing. He whistled a Christmas tune as he made the final wraps. "Ready for the unveiling?"

He plugged in the bottom light string and the tree twinkled with multi-colored LEDs. Clark began yawning as they hung the ornaments.

"Why don't you go to bed? You've been up since the crack of dark."

After a token resistance, he drained the dregs of his cocoa and went upstairs to their bedroom. Carolyn finished decorating the tree, then went into the kitchen to clean up after the cocoa making. As she was drying the cups, something thudded to the hardwood floor and small footfalls pattered across the room. *Hope Isobel doesn't take down the tree.* Carolyn had left the most fragile of the ornaments safe in their storage boxes.

She coaxed Knock and Brat outside for a final potty break and as soon as they came in from the cold, they burrowed underneath the blankets on their orthopedic beds.

"Goodnight, then. Don't let me keep you up," she said as she turned off the downstairs lights and went to hit the hay.

When Clark's alarm went off at 7:00, Carolyn got up with him. There were presents to wrap and pies to bake before they made the hour-long trip into the city for the party. Carolyn was able to work remotely four days a week, and Clark had sold off his budding tech startup for enough money to retire on 100 remote acres, or at least to hold him until he got his next business idea. Perhaps this month the pregnancy would take. It certainly wasn't from lack of trying.

She followed him downstairs. When she arrived in the kitchen, she had to lean against the doorframe.

"What on Earth?"

Clark came up behind her to peer over her shoulder.

The box of cocoa powder had been opened and not only was it spread all over the table, but the entire kitchen had been dusted in brown. A broken mug lay on the floor. The trash can had been tipped over and garbage scattered around the room.

"Must have been the cat," Clark said in Carolyn's ear.

She shook her head. "She only weighs three pounds. How would she pull that bin over? And she lacks opposable thumbs, so I don't know how she'd get the cocoa open."

"Well, I didn't do it, and the pups can't get on the table."

"Maybe they have a mischief pact, and all worked together."

Clark squeezed her shoulder. "I'll get the trash, you get the cocoa."

Carolyn hoped there would be enough cocoa left in the box for the chocolate chiffon pie she was planning to make as she wiped the table with a damp sponge. Clark stopped what he was doing and gazed at the floor, twisting his head this way and that.

"What's wrong?"

"Do any of our neighbors have small children?"

She moved to his side, and her eyes followed his. In the cocoa powder on the floor was the footprint of a small child. "I think the Hendersons have teenagers, and they're over a mile away. Don't know about the Molenas, but they're even farther, and I don't think a toddler would be able to cover that distance."

They both searched the linoleum, but they didn't find any other tracks.

❄ ❄ ❄

Carolyn and Clark stumbled in from the Dempsey's Christmas party around 3:30 AM. Clark had had a few too many cups of good cheer, and Carolyn had driven them home. He leaned against her for balance as she unlocked the door. The dogs did not meet them, as they always did.

"Brat? Knock?" she called and paused to listen for toenails clicking on tile.

There was only silence.

She called again for the dogs, but there was no response. Carolyn lead the staggering Clark forward into the great room and snapped on the light. "What?"

Every single ornament, save the Swarovski crystal star on top of the tree, had been thrown on the floor. A few were broken. The lights had been unplugged.

"Wow." Carolyn led Clark to the couch, and he plopped onto it. "Isobel must have had a field day while we were out. I'm too tired to worry about this now. I'll clean it up in the morning. Can you make it up the stairs?"

When there was no answer, she turned toward the sofa. Clark had already fallen asleep.

She left him where he was and went in search of the dogs. They were under the sofa in the den, and it was difficult to coax them out. She gave up and went to bed.

Carolyn fell into a restless sleep, troubled by nightmares of a grotesque creature, half troll and half porcupine chasing her through a foggy forest. Its oversized ears shook as it laughed at her terror, and the sharp quills that covered its back clicked together as it ran after her.

Sunlight streamed through the picture window when Carolyn awoke with a start. She was disoriented for a moment, but soon got her bearings and swung her feet over the edge of the bed to get up for the day. As she neared the closet, she heard plaintive mewing.

"Isobel? She opened the door, and the kitten came bounding out. *Ridiculous cat. Seems like after the third time of spending the night in the closet, you'd learn.*

Then she remembered the denuded Christmas tree. *If Isobel was locked in the closet...* "No," she said out loud. "I must have dreamed that. Just like the weird little man-thing chasing me."

When she made her way downstairs to put on the coffee, Clark was still snoring on the sofa. And the ornaments remained on the floor. She filled the coffeemaker. Daylight had emboldened the dogs, and they came into the kitchen to demand breakfast. Carolyn completed the feeding ritual and opened her laptop.

She began searching for information on poltergeists, but she wasn't sure that was the right answer. They'd had the house custom-built and moved in nine months ago. There were no burial grounds, native or otherwise, anywhere nearby. No adolescent children lived there—they seemed to be a common trigger for malicious ghost activity.

Wondering if the weird dream she'd had meant something, she queried 'half man half porcupine' and 'porcupine man,' but neither yielded results that fit her dream. Once she tried 'porcupine monster' and scrolled down the results page, however, she found herself looking at a creature remarkably similar to the one from her nightmare. It was called a pukwudgie.

Her excitement grew as she read the description. It was small, two to three feet tall, and lived in the forest. A shapeshifter, it could appear as a dangerous animal, like a cougar, but its normal form was something like a troll doll in front and a porcupine in back.

Pukwudgies had a long-standing grudge against humans and could be dangerous when provoked. *Today the ornaments, tomorrow it will be us broken on the floor? But why was it here? We've lived in this house with no problems for nine months. What's different now?*

The tree.

It started when we cut down that tree and brought it inside. Was it the pukwudgie's home? Maybe if they replaced it, the thing would go away. She went back to the great room and shook her husband awake.

"Clark. Get up. We have to go to a nursery."

"Who's having a baby?" he mumbled.

"A plant nursery, Clark. Get up."

He sat up and his eyelids drooped closed. He was worse than useless at this point.

She shook her head. "Nevermind. I'll do it myself. There's coffee in the pot."

Carolyn looked up the closest nursery that specialized in native plants.

Four hours and three nurserys later, Carolyn returned with an eight-foot loblolly pine. Clark was up and dressed when she walked through the front door, and he'd cleaned up the broken Christmas ornaments.

"Put your boots on, babe. I need you to help me plant a tree."

He squinted. "What?"

"I'll explain on the way. Come on."

She got a 5-gallon bucket and filled it three quarters of the way with water while he strapped the tree to the ATV.

"What is this about?" He climbed into the driver's seat.

"I think we stole the pukwudgie's home."

"The what?"

She explained her internet searches earlier in the day, as well as what a pukwudgie was. When she repeated her theory about the purloined pine, he shook his head, then rubbed his temples.

"Look. I get it if you feel guilty about cutting down a wild tree for Christmas. But I don't think for an instant that there's any such thing as a puckerwaj."

"Puck. Wudgie. Okay. Explain the ornaments getting thrown off the tree."

"The kitten."

"She was shut in my closet. How about the footprint in the cocoa?"

"It was... I don't know. But that doesn't mean porcupine people exist."

"Let's just plant the tree and see what happens, okay?"

He started the four-wheeler, and they drove down the trail to where they'd cut down the conifer. It took a little wandering to find the stump, but once they did, Clark brought the water and Carolyn dragged the tree. They planted it, gave it a good drink, and left.

When they returned to the house, Carolyn went into the great room and said, "Hello? Mr. or Mrs. Pukwudgie? I'm sorry if we stole your home. We planted you a new tree this afternoon. I hope it's as good as the old one."

Nothing unusual happened during the day. They wrapped family Christmas presents and played carols until they were both sick of holiday music.

Maybe that'll drive the Pukwudgie out, Carolyn mused. *If I hear one more version of 'Chestnuts Roasting on an Open Fire,' I'm going to leave.*

Carolyn was drifting off to sleep when something began tapping on the bedroom window. She tried to tell herself that it was just a tree branch, but she knew full well there were no trees that close to the upstairs window. She sat up and caught a glimpse of glowing yellow eyes peering into the bedroom. As soon as she sat up, they were gone. *Another dream?* She hardly slept the rest of the night.

The late-night window tapping continued for the next two nights. On Christmas morning, Carolyn could barely drag her sleep-deprived self out of bed. She put her sweater on backwards and grumbled as she turned it the right way around. *What did that thing want? They'd replaced the tree.*

She felt better after coffee and breakfast. She and Clark went into the great room to open the presents they'd bought for each other before they drove to his parents' house. Carolyn stared at the ornamentless pine tree. It wasn't entirely free of decoration—the star was still on top. She scowled and fetched the stepladder.

"What are you doing?" Clark asked. "I thought you wanted to open presents."

"I do. But I have to take care of something first." She snatched the star from the tree and marched outside.

Clark ran after her. "What are you doing?" He asked again, but more frantic this time.

"Come with me and you'll find out."

She drove the ATV to the newly planted pine and stopped. "You don't hear it—you could sleep through a bomb explosion. But it taps on the window at night and keeps me awake."

"What does?" He followed her to the tree.

"The pukwudgie. It wants something. A gift. I don't know. But it left the star on the tree when it pulled off all the decorations. So that's what I'm giving it."

"Really? You're gifting a $300 ornament to a thing that doesn't exist?"

"Yes." She stood on tiptoe and placed the glittering crystal star on the top of the loblolly. "It's yours now. Please let me sleep."

She drove them back in silence to the house. They had French toast and opened their presents. Carolyn put on the emerald tennis bracelet Clark bought her, and he put on the cashmere sweater she'd bought for him. They loaded the family presents into the car and left. Carolyn fell asleep almost immediately and awoke refreshed, albeit with a stiff neck, in her in-laws' driveway.

The holidays came and went. The nighttime tapping on the window stopped. Every time Carolyn went to water the newly planted pine, its starry crown sparkling in the dappled sunlight, she wondered if the pukwudgie was watching her, and hoped she never saw it again.

A Whip That Cracks

By Artemis Greenleaf

I REALLY hope you like it, Mom." Cheri handed over a small present wrapped in gold and red paper.

"Me, too." Frances pressed her thin lips together as she took the gift. She peeled off the paper, opened the box, and held up the pendant. "What is it?"

"It's a genuine Victorian jet piece. It's a locket, actually. I know it doesn't look like one." Hector said, moving closer to her. He ran a finger along the beaded edge of the pendant and pointed to the center. "This glyph is the letters 'A,' 'E,' and 'I,' all intertwined. Stands for Amity, Eternity, and Infinity. We replaced the existing picture with one of Cheri's dad. I can put it on you, if you'd like to wear it now."

Frances shrugged. Hector looked across the table at Cheri, who nodded.

He rose and unclasped the lobster claw hook on the chain, put the jewelry around his mother-in-law's neck, and re-clasped it. Hector sat back down and repositioned his napkin. "What do you think, Cheri?"

The waiter stopped to refill their tea. "That's beautiful. What a lovely Christmas gift."

"You don't need to butter *me* up." Frances jerked her head toward Hector. "He's the one paying the tip."

"Mother!" Cheri looked up at the embarrassed server. "Sorry about that. She's been through a lot lately."

He nodded and hurried away.

"I know this is your first Christmas without Dad. We all miss him. But it isn't the waiter's fault." She reached over and brushed a lock of brittle white hair off her mother's shoulder. "We were thinking we'd drive around a little and look at Christmas lights on the way back to the retirement home."

Frances shrugged, then shoveled a forkful of mashed potato into her mouth.

After dinner was finished and the check, with an extra-large holiday + cranky old lady tip, was paid, they waited under the portico while the valet fetched their car.

Cheri turned toward her husband. "Did I tell you I downloaded that app that shows the neighborhoods with the best lights?"

"Let's put it to good use." The smile slid off his face when his eyes met Frances'.

She stared blankly into the parking lot. "I think it's going to rain."

"We'll be in the car," Cheri assured her.

The valet pulled up and hopped out of the car. Hector handed him a twenty, because he felt anyone who worked on Christmas Eve deserved it.

Cheri started the app, and they began their tour of lights. In the first neighborhood, the entire cul-de-sac blazed with lights. She wondered if it could be seen from space. The house at the end had every square inch of surface area covered with LEDs. Santa waved from a sleigh in the front yard while elves loaded sacks into the back and Mrs. Claus presented a plate of cookies.

"Glad that's not my light bill," Frances muttered from the back seat.

"Well, there's that," Hector replied.

They were on the second to last neighborhood before the retirement village when Cheri tapped the screen on her phone.

"What's wrong?" Hector asked, braking to avoid a slow-moving herd of light-peepers.

"It says this house is extra special. Doesn't look like they even have any decorations."

"There's a bunch of people standing around. Let me turn around in this driveway and we'll sit here a bit and see if anything happens."

They sat in the dark for several minutes.

"Maybe they took it down." Hector reached for the shifter.

The roof erupted into fireworks. Unnoticed in the dark, a Jumbotron screen was fixed to the top of the house. After the fireworks dissipated, Santa's sleigh came in for a landing. A slapstick routine involving reindeer poop and the jolly old elf getting stuck in the sleigh ensued. Then a mish-mash of Christmas cartoons followed. Finally, it displayed a live-action nativity scene. After panning through the stable and showing the holy family, the wise men with their gifts, and the animals, the camera moved skyward, to the blazing star in the night sky that glittered above the scene. The star dissolved into various holiday greetings, and the screen went dark.

"Okay," Cheri said. "That was pretty amazing, don't you think so, Mom?"

When there was no reply, she twisted around to look at Frances. She leaned against the window, her head resting on her shoulder. Her mouth hung open, and a thread of drool hung all the way down to her coat.

A loud *snork* came from her throat, and she lolled her head back against the seat.

Cheri turned back to the front. "I guess we should just take her home now."

They walked Frances into her apartment. Cheri kissed her mother on the head. "We'll be at Hector's parents tomorrow, but we'll have you at our house for New Year's, remember."

Frances took off her coat. "I remember. Goodbye."

The couple closed the door behind them and walked toward their car.

Cheri was nearly in tears. "She's taking Daddy's death so hard. She used to love Christmas... New Year's... The whole holiday season. Even Halloween. This is awful. It's like she's dead, but her heart is still beating."

Hector rubbed her arm before he opened the car door for her. "Just give her time." He got in and started the engine. "Does she have any friends? Like ones we could invite for New Year's? That would probably perk her up."

"I don't think so. I believe they've all either died or moved to Florida."

A week later, Cheri and Hector arrived to pick Frances up. He knocked on the door.

"Come in, it's open," came from the video doorbell.

They stepped inside and Cheri's jaw dropped. Frances had been so depressed after her husband had passed that she'd been letting things go. The little apartment had become cluttered and dusty. The staff told Cheri that Frances wore the same clothes for days, and they often had to send someone to remind her to come eat dinner.

But the living room that greeted them was spotless, bordering on austere. Frances swept in from the bedroom. Her hair was pulled back into a French twist, and she wore a sparkly red sweater over her black skirt.

"I'm ready when you are," Frances grinned at them.

"I—I'm glad to see you're feeling better, Mom."

Frances turned her head, as if admiring the tidy room. "Yes. Ruth has been such a godsend. She's really been cracking the whip and helping me get it together."

"Ruth? You haven't spoken about her before, Mom. Does she live here?"

Frances picked up her purse and moved toward the door. "We met at Christmas. Don't want to be late to your own party, now do you?"

Since Frances had moved into the retirement village, Cheri had visited her mother every Friday, bringing groceries and sundries and often taking her out to dinner. Sometimes Hector came with her, sometimes not.

This particular Friday was the last one in January, and Hector had joined them. "Wow, Frances. You look amazing. You've colored your hair, changed your wardrobe. It's like a whole new you. Bet you've got suitors lined up around the block. We've got to meet this Ruth."

Frances fingered the jet pendant Cheri and Hector had given her. "Not interested in being courted by these old farts. Ruthie's out right now, I'm afraid. Have to be another time. Let's not keep that curry waiting."

The Thai food was delicious, and Frances made a pit stop before leaving. She spent such a long time in the ladies' room that Cheri became worried that she'd fallen.

Cheri pushed open the bathroom door. Each stall had its own full-sized door, so there was no way to check for feet or fallen bodies. The murmur of voices came from one stall.

"Mom? Frances?" Cheri called, her voice tentative.

The voices stopped. The toilet flushed and the door opened. Frances exited the stall with a broad smile.

"Who were you talking to in there?"

"Ruthie."

Cheri raised an eyebrow.

Frances banged her elbow against her purse as she washed hands. "On the phone."

"Okay. I was just worried when you didn't come back. That's all."

"I've never been better. In fact," Frances turned off the water. "Ruthie and I have been talking about taking a cruise in the spring. One of those huge, fancy ships to London."

"A cruise! I thought you hated boats."

"A cruise ship is different. You have to try new things sometimes, right? That's what you're always telling me."

The two women left the restroom and Hector met them by the hostess stand.

"What gorgeous eyes you have," Frances said to the valet.

"Thank you, ma'am." He hurried off to retrieve the car.

Hector and Cheri stared at each other in shock until their vehicle pulled up in front of them.

As they approached the retirement village, Cheri cleared her throat. "I probably should have gone to the bathroom at the restaurant. I really need to go now. You don't mind if we stop in for a minute, do you Mom?"

"I suppose not."

Cheri availed herself of the facilities while Hector remained in the living room with Frances. When she rejoined them, Hector looked ill.

"You okay, Babe? You look like you've seen a ghost."

"I'm fine. It's been great having dinner with you, Frances. Good night."

He barreled toward the door, Cheri in tow. "Night, Mom!"

As soon as they reached the car, Cheri stopped. "What is wrong with you? Why did you just barge out of my mother's house like that?"

"I'll tell you after we get home. I have to look up something first."

He gripped the steering wheel in white-knuckled silence the entire way home and trotted upstairs to his office as soon as they got through the front door.

A few minutes later, he called down. "Cheri? Come up here. You've got to see this."

She hurried up. "What is it?"

He handed her a small oval portrait. "This. This is Ruth."

Cheri frowned. "I don't understand."

"At your mom's house. There was reflection in the window. It was her." He tapped the photo. "It was Ruthie."

"Mom's been wearing her hair up a lot lately, and people don't use windows as mirrors for a reason. I'm sure it was just my mother you saw."

Hector shook his head. "No. She was in the kitchen."

Cheri gave him a skeptical tilt of the head. "Okay. Is there anything in the provenance about her? Where she lived? How she died?"

He shuffled through the papers on his desk. "Okay. The piece came from an estate sale... family heirloom...they were very wealthy...here's a newspaper clipping. Says here she drowned. Fell off a passenger vessel during a Trans-Atlantic crossing."

One Horse Open Slay

By A.B. Richards

CRANDALL James tugged at the dirty ribbed tank undershirt that drooped around his scrawny chest, stretching it out even more. "Don't know, Tessa. May as well just skip Christmas this year."

"But we always go to Mama and them's." Tessa wiped away a tear.

"I know, Sugarplum. But I don't got enough money to fill up the car, much less buy all them presents."

Her eyes narrowed. "I thought you said you was workin' an extra job."

"I am, but I ain't got paid yet."

Tessa eyed the array of empty beer bottles and overflowing ashtray on the coffee table. "Well, maybe Louise next door can drop us at the bus depot. I'm sure Mama'll understand if we cain't bring nothin' this year."

"Is your cousin Virgil gonna be there?"

"Well, he usually is, ain't he?"

Crandall slurped his beer. "You know how he always spends so much on presents. Be pretty embarassin' if we show up empty-handed."

"You're just lookin' for excuses not to go, now."

He set down his drink. "Sugar, come on. You know that ain't true."

"Do I?"

"Okay. Okay. I'll figger something out. I'm just gonna go for a walk to clear my head."

He grabbed his third-hand bomber jacket and stalked out of the house, the screen door slapping against the frame in his wake. The late afternoon shadows stretched across the road, chilling any warmth from the meager sun.

The thrumming of a diesel engine got louder, coming up behind him as he walked along the weedy edge of the road. When the cab was even with Crandall, the window rolled down.

"Get in, loser!"

Crandall opened the door and climbed in. "You were s'posed to meet me at The Hideout, Bobby. Not here."

"I'd be sittin' there for twenty minutes waitin' on your sorry ass to show up."

"Well, Tessa prob'ly ain't gonna see us anyway. This'll be a Christmas she'll never forget. Guaranteed."

"Sounds like you got a plan."

"I do. Let's grab a beer or three and I'll tell you all about it."

The greasy remains of two burger baskets sat between Crandall and Bobby on the back table at The Hideout Bar & Grill, nestled in a forest of empty beer bottles.

Bobby wiped his nose on his sleeve. "I don't know if that's gonna work, dude."

"Course it will. We gotta find a good place for a stakeout, then when the opportunity strikes—and there will be plenty—we move in and boom! Done. I'll be on the inside, and I'll text you when I'm on the way out. All you gotta do is meet me at the car with the gun." He snickered as he shook his head. "Never see it comin'."

"Seems risky." Bobby took another swig of beer. "And you only got three days."

"Yep. Should prob'ly go do some reconnoiterin' this evenin'."

They rode in silence to the Northland Heights mall, one town over, on the fancy side of the tracks. Luxury cars circled the congested parking lot like low-flying vultures. Those lucky enough to snag a spot in this automotive game of musical chairs trickled into the mall. Another group, laden with bags and packages, streamed out.

Crandall patted the dash. "Told ya. Perfect. Let's go in, have a look around."

Bobby found a parking spot three blocks away, and they made their way back to the mall, keeping an eye out for security cameras.

"You got one of them ski masks or somethin', right, Bobby?"

"Nah. But I got a werewolf mask from Halloween."

"Long as they can't see your face."

On the next night, Crandall hopped into Bobby's truck at the end of the block. He'd showered and put on clean clothes.

Bobby grinned. "Tessa's gonna think you're steppin' out on her."

Crandall grinned back. "Not for long, she won't."

They avoided the busy parking lot altogether, parking in the same spot they'd scoped out earlier. It would be easy to slip into the crowd of harried holiday shoppers and enter the mall.

"I'm gonna find her. You just be ready." Crandall left Bobby shivering in the parking lot, werewolf mask crumpled under his jacket.

Crandall sat on a bench near the main entrance and waited. There she was. The perfect mark, talking on her phone and not paying attention. He trailed some distance behind her, watching.

Expensive jewelry.

Designer clothes.

Fancy gadgets.

Alright, Cousin Virgil! Wait 'til you get a load of this.

Crandall had to stop himself from rubbing his hands together with delight as he followed the woman in the red blouse from store to store. He loitered at the windows and pretended to look at displays as she made her purchases. A couple of times he hid behind kiosks when she surveyed her surroundings.

When the woman in red exited an expensive cookware boutique, she was on her phone. "Yeah, yeah. I'm on my way. See you soon. Don't do anything until I get there. It's done. I've got the packages."

Crandall pulled out his phone and messaged Bobby. "Red shirt. Brown hair."

"Got it," Bobby messaged back.

Following at a safe distance, Crandall watched her click the remote to a large Mercedes sedan. The lights came on and the trunk slowly opened. He hurried his steps to catch up with her, but the open lid blocked his view. He pulled a red bandana up over his nose.

There was a little yelp as he rounded the corner. Bobby had just shown up with his werewolf mask, waving a pistol.

Crandall cut off her escape, noting with glee that the trunk was stuffed with packages wrapped in black plastic in addition to the loot she just put in there. He'd hit the jackpot this time.

Suck it, Cousin Virgil.

"Just give us your keys and purse, and you won't get hurt," Bobby growled.

The woman stared into the trunk and swallowed. "Okay."

Crandall snatched the key fob with one hand and the Coach bag with the other, then jumped into the driver's seat. Bobby got in on the passenger side. Tires squealed as they tore out of the parking space. Crandall watched the woman in the rear-view mirror. Her hand covered her mouth and her shoulders shook.

"Sorry lady," Bobby mumbled.

"Don't worry none about her. She got plenty of insurance."

"Yeah, but it don't feel right, makin' a lady cry."

He dropped Bobby at his truck, and they took the backroads to Bobby's house. They parked the Mercedes in his barn and Crandall went through the purse, checking for cash. He turned the cell phone off and took out the battery.

"Where'd you put that GPS blocker, Bobby?"

"Hold up. I'll get it—it's in the house."

A few minutes later, Bobby returned with a small device. He paused and whistled at the sleek machine. "We should get some different plates. Same kinda car, though."

"Not too many white Mercedeses out here, dingus."

"Bet we could find some at the mall or thereabouts."

❄ ❄ ❄

Tessa gaped at the white Mercedes in the driveway.

"Told ya I'd figger somethin' out, Sugarplum. I just… borrowed it."

"From who?"

"Betty Samaritan. Real nice lady. Told ya I been working a part-time job doin' handyman stuff. She asked me what we was doin' for Christmas and when I told her nothin', 'cause my old car wasn't gonna make it to your mama's, she handed her keys right over.

She got six more cars, so it don't make no difference to her to lend one out."

Tessa buckled herself into the luxurious seat. "What about presents?"

"Trunk's loaded up with 'em."

Crandall grinned the whole way to Tessa's mama's house, savoring the look that would be on Cousin Virgil's face when he clapped eyes on that white Mercedes.

Tessa sang along to Christmas songs on the radio for the whole trip, and. The entire family came out onto the front porch when they saw that car coming up the drive.

Cousin Virgil was the first to speak. "Crandall James! Where on Earth did *you* get that machine?"

Tessa was busy hugging the relatives.

Crandall smirked as he clicked a button on the remote. "Why don't you help me bring in the presents? Didn't have time to get 'em all wrapped, though."

Virgil's nose wrinkled. "I think your potluck has gone bad."

It hadn't occurred to Crandall that the woman might have had perishable groceries in the trunk. *Oh, well. Win some, lose some.*

He handed an Hermes shopping bag to Virgil, reached for one of the black packages, and peeled off the tape to peek inside.

"Sweet Baby Jesus!" Virgil gasped.

A hand, attached to a hairy forearm, fell out of the package and tumbled onto the ground.

Crandall hung his head. *That bitch. She wasn't cryin' when we left her in the parking lot. She was laughin'. At me.*

Stalking in a Winter Wonderland

By Holly Dey

ROSE Donovan tried not to recoil in horror.

"I know Mama woulda wanted you to have her. She said you're the only one who loved Melinda as much as she did."

Loved her? That's what I get for tryin' to be polite. "Well, Kathy. That's awful sweet of you, honey. But I just can't imagine your Christmas without her. She's… well, she's like part of your family. I'm sure your kids look forward to seein' their meemaw's Melinda every Christmas."

Kathy shook her head rapidly. "Actually, they're terrified of her."

Why am I not surprised? "They're just little. I'm sure they'll grow out of it."

"Please, Mrs. Donovan? Please take Melinda."

Trey Donovan came out of the kitchen, a mug of spiced apple cider in his hand, and strolled up to the front door.

"Hey, Kathy. You doin' okay? That sure was a nice service they had for your mama. Oh. I see you got that cree—Christmas doll. Supposed to be Mrs. Claus, isn't it?"

"Yes, sir. I was just telling Mrs. Donovan here that Mama really would have wanted her to have Melinda. She needs someone who can handle, I mean take care of, her."

Trey slipped his free arm around Rose's waist. "Of course. If it's that important to you. We'll take her in."

Kathy's eyes lit up and her shoulders relaxed as she handed the four-foot doll over to Trey. "Thank y'all so much. You have a good Christmas, now."

She hurried away before the Donovan's had a chance to reconsider.

Rose regarded the doll in her husband's arms. Melinda should have been darling. She wore a cheerful Christmas red, green, white, and gold plaid dress with a lacy crocheted collar and a white apron. Her grey hair was braided and coiled into a bun atop her head. Bright blue glass eyes peered out from behind round wire-rimmed spectacles.

But there was something wrong with her face.

No blatant disfigurations. No large cracks or marring. Nothing Rose could put her finger on, really. Craquelure of the antique paint on her porcelain skin had drawn a spider's web of fine lines across her cheeks and forehead, but that wasn't the problem. She was just... uncanny. But it was also true that Rose felt that way about dolls in general, so maybe it wasn't solely on Melinda.

"Mama!" Daisy, the middle Donovan child, shouted. "Rocky's eatin' all the popcorn!"

Rose and Trey looked at each other and said, nearly in unison, "Every year."

"I'll take care of it. You do something with her." Rose's eyes fell on the doll, and she shuddered before turning around to face her children in the living room behind her.

Primrose, the eldest at fifteen, sat on the loveseat, earphones plugged into her Sony Walkman, listening to a cassette tape while she serenely strung cranberries and popcorn on a length of kitchen twine.

Eleven-year-old Rocky was on his knees in front of the table, cheeks puffed out like a foraging chipmunk with a mother-lode of seeds.

Rose gestured to the extra-large mixing bowl, about three-quarters full of popcorn. "Daisy, honey, there's plenty of popcorn. You know I always make extra. Some for you, some for the birds."

Daisy drooped. "I know, Mama. But he gets his slobber on it and makes it soggy."

Ewww. "I see. Rocky, why don't you go get yourself a bowl for the popcorn you're eatin', okay, honey?"

"Oh hay, haha," Rocky said as he got to his feet.

"Don't talk with your mouth full," Rose called after him as he power-walked out of the room to fetch a bowl.

A high-pitched shout came from the kitchen. Rocky nearly bowled Rose over as he pelted into the living room.

"Honey, what's wrong?"

"M-m-monster."

Now Primrose and Daisy flanked their mother.

"A monster?" Primrose asked. "No such thing, Rock."

Trey hustled in from the back porch. "What happened?"

Daisy piped up, smirking. "Rocky said he saw a monster in the kitchen."

"I didn't see any monsters when I came in just now." He flipped on the light, then startled. "I forgot about Melinda. I wouldn't say she's a monster, though."

The large doll stood at the back of the kitchen, near the door to the porch.

Rocky sniffled. "Why did you get a creepy doll?"

"She's not… supposed to be creepy," Rose explained. "You remember Mrs. McCall? She was your Sunday School teacher when you were in third grade?"

"Yes."

"Well, she passed away last week, and her daughter wanted me to have Melinda. The Mrs. Claus doll."

"I don't like her," Rocky replied.

"You're scared of a doll?"

"Knock it off, Daisy." Rose fixed her younger daughter with a warning look.

Daisy sulked back to the couch to continue her garland making, Primrose not far behind her.

Rose leaned toward Rocky and whispered, "I think she's creepy, too. But she's just a doll. Not sure what to do with her, but we'll figure something out."

The children had gone to bed and Rose was putting away the supper dishes. Trey sat at the table, scribbling on a piece of paper. The flap on the pet door slapped against its frame.

"Trey, would you let Merlin in?"

He set his pencil down and got up to open the back door. A large black cat with golden eyes and a patch of white on his chest waited on the screened-in back porch.

"Come on, let's get you your dinner."

Merlin stepped over the threshold and froze. He stared at Melinda and hissed, then turned tail and ran back out to the porch.

Rose sighed. "He never did take kindly to strangers. Why don't you just put his food out there for him? It's not that cold out and he's got plenty of fur."

Trey fed the cat and returned to the table. Rose closed the cabinet after the last cereal bowl had been put away and took a seat across from him.

"What is it you wanted to talk about, Trey?"

He tapped his pencil on his paper and ran his tongue over his teeth. "Well. You know my unemployement's about to run out." He shook his head. "Two years ago, people were standing in line on odd or even days for gasoline that might not last until it was their turn. Now, we have an oil glut and nobody's drillin' anymore, trying to scale back production to get prices up. I've applied for jobs as far away as Houston, Austin, and even Dallas. Seems like these days, a petroleum engineer can't get arrested, much less hired."

Rose picked at her thumbnail. "I can take on more hours at Marberger's."

"I don't want you to do that. Being a grocery check-out girl barely pays anything, anyway. But I have an idea."

"As long as it ain't illegal, immoral, or fattenin'."

Trey chuckled softly and smiled at his wife before rotating the paper and pushing it across the table toward her. "Hear me out. You know Josette Freestone wants to sell the ShopStop and retire."

"I'd heard that."

"I wanna buy it."

"What do *you* know about runnin' a convenience store?" Rose chewed her lip.

"That's an excellent question. I, uh, talked to Josette. She said she'd be willing to stay around for a couple of months to teach me the ropes."

Rose leaned back in her chair and crossed her arms. "You've already made up your mind."

He shook his head. "Rose, this isn't the 1950s. I'm not going to make a unilateral decision. You've got to be fully on board, or this'll never work. There's a lot of good reasons, aside from the fact I can't find a job. I'll be closer to home, and I can spend more time with the kids, instead of commuting forty-five minutes each way.

I'll never get laid off again, and we have the chance to be masters of our own fate. I can use some of my layoff money for the down payment. I've run several scenarios in VisiCalc. Let me show you."

Rose's eyelids snapped open, and she held her breath, listening intently in the dark. Next to her, Trey's breathing was slow and deep. The clock read 3:02.

The noise came again from the kitchen. *Something falling on the linoleum? Perhaps Trey had let Merlin in before he came to bed.*

It was probably just the cat, but she wouldn't be able to sleep unless she knew for sure. Rose got out of bed as quietly as she could so as not to wake Trey and slipped into the kitchen. She snapped on the light. At first, nothing seemed amiss, but then she noticed that Melinda was lying on the floor. Rose took a step toward her, but stopped.

If she fell over once, she'll fall over again. May as well leave her there until the morning so she doesn't keep waking me up.

She made a pitstop in the bathroom before snuggling back into bed. Lying on her side, she stared at the wall. Rose was terrified at the prospect of buying the ShopStop. They didn't know anything about running a business. But they had to do something. His unemployment checks would stop coming after next month.

As she stared, darkness began to collect on the wall. If formed into a roughly human shape, although much taller. She gasped through her teeth. The apparition didn't come any closer, just stood there, watching, darker than dark against the wall.

She shrank back against Trey, who mumbled something and flopped his arm over her waist.

The shadow remained.

It's just your imagination because you're stressed right now. She pulled the blanket over her head and eventually went back to sleep.

Rose yawned and blinked at the pale sunlight filtering through the edges of the blinds. A glance at the clock told her it was just after eight. She panicked for a moment before remembering that it was the Christmas holidays—no one was going to school today. Trey was already up. She stretched and swung her feet over the side of the bed.

The percolator gurgled in the kitchen. Sunlight and the smell of coffee chased away the remains of the night shadows. Rose smiled as she got dressed, going over her Christmas Eve eve checklist in her head. When she went to work this afternoon, she'd pick up the few forgotten items she'd need to prepare their Christmas feast.

Primrose was just coming in through the back door, wiping her hands on her jeans.

"You're out and about early, honey."

"Just feedin' the chickens."

Rose tilted her head. "Why isn't Rocky doin' that?"

"He and Daddy went off somewhere. Asked me to feed 'em"

"I see. I don't suppose they said where they were goin'?"

Primrose shook her head.

Rose popped some bread into the toaster. Her eyes searched the back wall. Melinda was nowhere in sight. *Maybe they took her to the dump.*

Disappointment washed over her when she stepped into the living room and saw the doll propped between the wall and the Christmas tree.

Rose drained the pasta into a colander. The phone on the wall rang and Daisy trotted in to pick it up.

"Donovan Residence... Hold on... Rosie! It's your boooyfrieeeend."

Primrose hurried into the kitchen and snatched the receiver from her sister, who giggled.

"Dinner's almost ready," Rose mouthed at her daughters.

Daisy skipped out of the kitchen. Primrose turned away from her mother. "Hey, Woody."

Rose had other things on her mind and tried not to eavesdrop on her daughter's conversation. Trey and Rocky had gone to her brother's house to pick up a wild turkey he'd shot. They'd dressed the bird while they were at Raymond's place, so all Rose had to do was try and figure when to start brining it.

She poured the pasta back into the pot and stirred in some olive oil, then set plates and silverware on the counter.

"Dinner's ready!" Rose leaned out of the door into the living room.

And shuddered.

Melinda's head was turned toward the kitchen. The blinking lights on the tree alternately lit up her face in unnatural colors and cast sinister shadows on it.

Rose blocked the doorway with her body. "Who did that?"

Trey's brow furrowed. "Did what?"

No one took credit.

Once again, Rose's eyes snapped open. Once again, the clock read 3:02. There was no shadow, but something scratched at the bedroom door.

Merlin?

The cat hadn't returned since he fled the kitchen the night before.

Rose slipped out of bed, forcing her feet to take each step. She held her breath, and with a trembling hand, flung open the door.

Nothing was there.

She padded into the living room. Melinda stood at the front window, moonlight casting her in silhouette, with a long shadow behind her.

Rose swallowed hard and crept back to bed. *One of the kids is trying to prank me. That's all. Bet it's Rocky. Maybe not. He was scared of the doll. Daisy?*

She snuggled against Trey's warm body and drifted back to sleep, dreaming strange dreams about running through the woods at night.

The jangling of the phone woke her at a quarter of six. The blocky device sat on her nightstand, and she fumbled with the receiver. "Hello?"

"Mrs. Donovan. If you didn't want Melinda, you could have just said no."

"Kathy? What are you talking about?"

"She's here, Mrs. Donovan. On my front porch. Where you left her."

"I did no such thing! She was in the living room when I went to bed last night."

"Oh." Kathy's voice was hardly more than a squeak.

Rose yawned. "You could… I don't know. Donate her to the museum. That new history teacher at the high school, what's his name?" She wracked her brain. "Tom Wharton. He's working with the historical society. Why don't you give him a call and see if they'll take it?"

"Thanks. I'm sorry."

"It's alright."

About 2:00 in the afternoon, Rose was out in the yard picking some fresh sage leaves when she noticed a plume of black smoke rising from somewhere in town. She called her friend Imogene to see if she'd heard anything.

"Oh, yeah. Kathy Patterson's house caught fire. Seems like they were tryin' to burn somethin' in the fireplace, and some embers fell out onto the carpet. Should have done that outside, that's for sure."

"Kathy. Patterson. Wow. That's awful at any time, but on Christmas Eve?"

"I know. Firefighters'll be out there for a while. Hope they're able to save the house."

"Me, too."

Rose hung up.

She got her turkey brining and then drove over to Kathy's house. The family was huddled on the curb, faces sooty and tear streaked.

Melinda leaned against a fire hydrant on the corner.

As Rose hurried past her, she noticed that the doll was spotless.

And then Melinda winked at her.

The Silent Stars Go By
By A.B. Richards

A N artificial evergreen forest sprouted from the deck of the cruise ship, and glittering green wreaths hung from the bulkheads.

"Who knew they had a Christmas cruise?" My mother craned her head to take in the artificial snow that drifted beneath the twinkling trees.

"Happy anniversary!" My sister squeezed her husband's hand.

"That Christmas wedding doesn't seem like such a bad idea, after all, now does it?" I asked.

"Fifty anniversaries, fifty Christmases. I never thought it was a bad idea, Eleanor." My dad slipped his arm around my mom's waist.

"Oh, Tom." She leaned into him and planted a tiny kiss on his cheek.

My sister, Laci, and Jordan, her husband, had engineered the holiday cruise as a fiftieth Christmaversary present for Mom and Dad. They had outvoted my desire for something on dry land. But I couldn't break my parents' hearts by missing the celebration, even if it meant stepping foot on a boat, let alone one on the open ocean, where things could go very wrong, very quickly, and help was not nearby.

A perky young woman in a white nautical uniform, nametagged 'Jani,' showed us to our suites and gave us a copy of the schedule. We were at the captain's table for dinner on the third night of a six-night cruise. There were only two stops, Cozumel and Costa Maya, and she warned us that if we wanted to go ashore, we should book our activities as early as possible. Jani led us through the maze to our accommodations and wished us well. I was grateful for the map she left with us, but maybe a ball of string would have been helpful.

Our two suites slept three each, connected by a double-sized living room. I chose the pull-out sofa bed farther from the Christmas tree. I opened the door and stepped out onto the balcony. The harbor water was murky, and trash floated near the dock. Chilly rain began to sprinkle on my head, so I went back inside. I wasn't normally one to believe in omens and portents, but that seemed like misfortune smacking me upside the head to announce its arrival.

I found the map and studied the route to the lifeboats. Just in case.

"Shall we go out and wander around on the decks?" my father asked.

"It's raining," I replied.

"Oh." Mom's shoulders dropped.

"I'm sure that rain won't follow us to Mexico." Jordan pasted a smile on his face. "All the shows and the restaurants will be inside—may as well go get the lay of the land, so to speak."

"May as well." *Unless you want to just sit around here looking at each other.*

Mom made sure we all had our cruise cards and maps before we set out on our recon mission while we waited for Laci to finish a call to her youngest daughter. She'd just had another baby, and their three-year-old needed some GamGam time.

I never had kids, but Laci and Jordan's kids had kids, all of whom were too little to enjoy a cruise. I kind of missed seeing them, actually. Normally, we all got together at Mom and Dad's house for Christmas. This year, we were cruising, and they were at Mom and Dad's, taking care of the dogs and chickens. Honestly, I felt relieved they were not on this boat. Not because they were babies. Because they were safe. Safe from deep water that crushed lungs and teemed with hungry, toothy mouths.

Laci disconnected, and we set off in search of entertainment. Jordan went straight to the casino. It was shuttered until the ship was in international waters. Gambling wasn't my thing—I'd keep my eyes peeled for the theaters. Nearly all the amenities were either on the top four and bottom three decks, with the other seven levels almost exclusively staterooms.

Counting from the top, we were at the thirteenth deck. I started for the stairs, but a woman holding an umbrella drink said, "Oh, you don't want to go down there."

"Why?"

"Nothing to see. Just the medical center." She took a sip of her drink. "And they have a morgue. Did you know they have morgues on cruise ships? I had no idea."

I knew but preferred not to think about it.

We returned to the shops on this deck. I peered in the window of a fine arts gallery.

Dad patted his stomach. "May as well have lunch while we're down here. Still another two hours before our... what was it that girl called it? A mustard drill?"

Laci rolled her eyes. "You're just hungry, Dad. It's a muster—no 'd'—drill."

Lunch was superb. I felt better having seen the lifeboats with my own two eyes during the muster drill. It was early, but I was tired, and I would have been happy enough to have gone back to the stateroom, put my feet up, and read a book. But Mom said we should go up to the top deck and wave goodbye as the boat got underway.

We took the elevator to the top deck. The drizzle had stopped, but it was chilly, and everything was wet. I felt dumb waving to the small cluster of people behind the fence at the terminal, none of whom I knew.

The next night, we had sailed more than halfway to Mexico, and we'd settled on the main dining room for dinner. We had devoured our entrees and were about to hit the dessert table when people started shouting. We all got to our feet, lookie-loos that we were, and saw a man who had collapsed face-first into his meal. Some of his tablemates resettled him to the floor and wiped the food off his face. He didn't look that old, maybe fifty-ish with salt-and-pepper hair. A bumpy roman nose gave his face character. His eyes were closed.

Paramedics arrived in no time. They tried CPR and a defibrillator, but after a while, the one who appeared to be in charge shook his head. They put the man on a stretcher and wheeled him away. I wondered how much use the morgue got on a typical cruise.

The mood of the dining crowd turned somber. We skipped dessert. Laci and Jordan went to the casino while Mom, Dad, and I returned to the suites. We all went to bed. My sister and BIL returning at 1 AM woke me. I tossed and turned, but no amount of readjusting my position would summon Morpheus. I gave up and decided to see what was happening around the ship.

The nightclub on the elevated deck was heaving. I went downstairs. There was no one near the pool. Or so I thought. I turned a corner near the fitness center entrance and bumbled into a romantically engaged couple. Mumbling apologies, I stepped back. The taller of the two—I assumed it was the man, but couldn't swear to it—fled, dropping his partner like a sack of potatoes.

She lay on the deck, clutching her throat and whimpering. I ran to her, grabbing my phone to use as a flashlight. I almost dropped it when the light hit her. She was covered in the blood that dripped from a ragged wound at the base of her throat.

I screamed.

No one came running. This lady needed help, or she wasn't going to make it. I swept my phone light around and caught a glimpse of red. I nearly tripped over a deck chair as I raced to pull the fire alarm. That should get somebody up here on the double.

I ran back to the woman and helped her put pressure on her wound. As I expected, crew members swarmed our location. They got the medical staff, who whisked the woman away on a gurney.

I told the security officers what I saw, which wasn't much. They took down my name and stateroom number, in case they had more questions.

What kind of freak does that? Obviously, a vampire. But vampires aren't real. There are people who *think* they're vampires, though. Now it seems there's some delusional psychopath on the ship. No way I was going to be able to sleep now. I went to the upper deck, where it was more peopley, and looked at the icy stars that twinkled above the fake evergreen garlands that wrapped the railings. Things that hunted at night swam in the black water beneath us, and one stalked the ship.

I started yawning as grey seeped above the eastern horizon, so I made my way back to the suite to see if I could nab some shut eye before the others began stirring.

Mom poked me in the ribs at 7:30. "Wake up lazybones. You're the last one up, Lana. Everyone's hungry, and we don't want to miss our Cozumel tour."

Bleary-eyed, I brushed my teeth and put my swimsuit on under my clothes. After a walking/shopping tour, we had a snorkeling excursion planned.

I had never snorkeled before. My body rebelled when I tried to breathe with my face in the water. It took several tries, but I finally got used to it. We all had life vests and floated in water that was too shallow for big boats, but at least twice as deep as any of us were tall.

A grey stingray undulated by as we looked on. Our guide waved to get our attention. He pointed to a strange fish, about two feet long, with markings that looked a bit like a chain-link fence. Hence the name 'chain catshark.' I recognized it from the brochure Mom had handed out on the ship when we were shopping for activities.

When I woke up from my nap, Mom asked me to go find Jordan at the casino because it was time to get ready for our dinner with the captain. Laci was taking rollers out of her hair and Dad was in the shower.

I took the elevator and got off on the casino's deck. As I walked toward the entrance, I couldn't shake the feeling I was being watched. I paused twice to look around, but didn't see anyone staring at me.

Jordan was at a craps table and had a decent pile of chips in front of him, although I had no idea how many he started with. A young woman in a red dress stood next to him and kept touching his arm. He'd take a step away and she fill in the distance. My BIL picked up his chips, and the woman tried to take his arm.

When his eyes fell on me, his face lit up. "Lana! Is it time?"

He rushed toward me and as soon as I got within range, he linked his arm through mine and kissed me on the cheek. "Let's go."

"You seem to have a fan club."

He rolled his eyes. "Not sure if she's digging for gold or just lonely. But she's been working her way around the tables."

The captain's dinner was very elegant. The food was beautiful to look at, although I personally found some of the flavor combinations off-putting. Wasabi potatoes and parsnip puree with jalapeno mince didn't appeal, so I had a salad. Can't go wrong with a salad.

I wanted to ask about the woman who'd been attacked last night, but figured it was a bad idea. Nothing had been said about it in the morning at breakfast. Since we'd been out all day, I don't know if there was any mention of it at lunch. I spotted one of the medics at another table and hoped I could buttonhole him before we went back to our suite.

Sadly, he slipped out before I could work my way over to him. After my power nap, I had re-energized and wasn't ready for bed, so I asked Laci if she wanted to go to the lounge with me. Mom and Dad went to the stateroom and me, Laci, and Jordan had a few drinks. I still wasn't tired when my sister started yawning. She and Jordan went to the room and left me on my lonesome. It was midnight, my normal bedtime, but I wasn't ready to sleep.

I wandered out to the upper deck and looked up at the stars. There isn't nearly as much light pollution off the shore of Cozumel as there is at our starting point of Galveston. I couldn't begin to count the stars, and the few constellations that I could normally pick out were lost in a crowded field of sparkling sky.

I peered over the railing. Blue globs swayed and drifted in the water below. I had read about this—it was bioluminescent phytoplankton. But they looked like their very own galaxy floating and twisting under the water.

Was that a noise behind me? I turned but saw nothing. *You're just tired*, I told myself. There were some deck chairs a little further away from the lighted club entrance, so I went over there. I could stretch out and watch the sky a little longer before my day caught up with me and I had to rest.

Some of the chairs were clustered together, so I moved one.

And found a foot.

A red stiletto shoe encased the foot. I moved the other chairs, and I didn't even need to turn on my phone to see that it was the lady in red who'd been hitting on Jordan. A dark stain covered her shoulder, and I didn't want to look. I took off my heels and ran to the bar, which was closest, to get help.

The security officers were suspicious, given that I found one injured girl and one dead one. I explained that I just wanted to watch the stars, so I went to the least populated areas of the ship. Which is also where someone looking to hide a body would go, so it made perfect sense that we'd end up in the same places.

They didn't look like they believed me. But I was wearing the same outfit from dinner at the captain's table and there wasn't a drop of blood on it, so they were going to have a tough time connecting me to her. Besides, there had to be camera footage of me, Laci, and Jordan in the bar. I'd only been out wandering around for a few minutes.

Exhaustion washed over me then, and I wanted nothing more than to go to bed. I crept in, trying not to wake anyone, and stripped off my itchy sequin dress right there in the living room before putting on the nightgown that was tucked into my pillowcase. I curled into a fetal position under the covers and started to cry. I cried for the two young women who'd been attacked. I cried for the man who died the second night of the trip. I cried for the danger Mom, Laci, and I could be in. From now on, we should never go anywhere alone.

Puffy eyes notwithstanding, I felt better when the morning sun chased the shadows away. We had the day in Costa Maya, then we'd be headed back home. There were two nights left to get through.

We opted not to swim with the dolphins, but watched them for a while. As we wandered around the port, there was a shop selling *alebrijes*—hand-carved, colorful Mexican folk-art monsters. Some were chimeras, like a donkey with butterfly wings, or an armadillo crossed with a coral snake. Others were animals with exaggerated features, like the rabbit with ears three times their normal size and huge eyes.

I hadn't planned to buy one, but there was a dragon I had to have. From its butterfly wings to its lizard body, it was blue, yellow, orange, green, and white. A long polka dotted tail tapered to a sharp point behind it. There was something both fierce and whimsical about the creature that I found irresistible. The sales lady had smiled when she rang up my order. The dragon would chase away evil spirits, she told me. Probably says that to everybody.

There was a long pier between Costa Maya and the cruise ship, and we were among the last to return to the boat. Dad was hangry, so we stopped to eat in one of the smaller restaurants, thinking it would be less busy than the main dining area. After the meal, Mom and Dad went back to the suite.

Laci and I sat in the bar and chatted while Jordan went to the casino. We took out our *alebrijes* and compared them. She'd gotten a seahorse that was just stunning. It had rows of bright designs in intricate patterns—made me think of a zentangle—in all the colors. I was still happier with my dragon.

My sister got up to go to the ladies' room, and I sat there on purse patrol. I was casually looking around the room.

That's when I saw him.

It could not have been him, but there he was. Salt-and-pepper hair. Bumpy roman nose. The guy who died on the second night of the cruise. He saw me and a smile spread over his face as he made his way over.

"Hi," he said. "I'm Derrick."

I could not stop staring into his eyes. They were a mesmerizing silvery blue.

"Hi. Derrick."

"It's nice to meet you, Lana."

Did I tell him my name? No, I don't think so. "Yes."

"Would you like to go on the upper deck and look at the stars?"

Everything in my brain screamed *No! Don't do it! Stay right here!* But I got up, still clutching my dragon, and said, "Sure."

We went to a lonely corner, and he turned to face me, putting a hand on each shoulder. When I looked into his eyes this time, they were every bit as hypnotic but red. I think I wanted to run, but I couldn't look away.

The man caressed my jaw, then tilted my head a little before nuzzling my neck. As soon as the eye contact broke, I gained a small amount of volition.

"I don't understand. You're dead. How can you be here?"

He stroked my hair as he whispered in my ear. "I think the term you're looking for is 'undead.' Pretty easy to fake your own death when you've got no heartbeat."

"But why would you want to do that?"

He chuckled. "Well, if I'm dead and in the morgue, no one is going to suspect me, now, are they? I'm free as a bird to do as I like."

Derrick bared his teeth, and I saw abnormally long canines, sharpened to a point. I kept my gaze on his mouth. Anywhere but his eyes.

I stepped back and used the only weapon I had. My dragon *Alebrije*. I stabbed him with the pointy tail. There must have been some good luck charm on it or something, because the tail went straight for the heart.

He blinked a few times, rapidly, and coughed.

Then he shattered into a million sparkling pieces of dust.

The ocean breeze swirled some of them around the deck and into the ocean. This was a thing that couldn't happen, but it just did. I didn't know what to think, so I went back to the table in the bar and sat down.

Laci looked up. "Where have you been? If I had realized you were going to run off and leave my purse..."

"I'm sorry. Couldn't be helped. Everything's still in there, though, right?"

"Looks like it. Listen, it's been great talking to you. I love seeing you at the holidays. But I need to go to bed."

"Night, Sis."

Now that the danger had passed, I felt safer being alone on the deck at night. Maybe the whole thing was just a weird dream, and no one had died. I even went to an unpopulated corner, where I sat and watched the stars go by.

Sad Tidings We Bring

By A.B. Richards

Victoria Parker squinted through the peephole. It was almost 11 PM, awfully late for visitors, especially in a raging thunderstorm. The two men on her covered porch wore the khaki uniforms of state troopers.

What on earth do they want?

She opened the door a crack. "May I help you?" she shouted over the downpour.

One of them fidgeted with the cowboy hat in his hands. "Are you Victoria Parker?"

"Yes?"

"May we come inside, please?"

"What's this about?"

"It might be better if we came inside."

"What are you, Black-Eyed Kids? No. Unless you have a warrant, you tell me what you need to tell me from out there."

One trooper shared a look with the other, then back to Victoria. "Ma'am, I regret to inform you that your husband has been killed in a traffic accident."

She blinked rapidly a few times. "I'm sorry. There must be some mistake."

"No, ma'am. I'm afraid not."

"You are married to Allen Parker?" The second officer asked.

"Yes, but—"

"I'm sorry for your loss, ma'am," the first trooper replied. "There's a chaplain on the way."

A bolt of lightning shattered the dark, and the thunder in its wake shook the house. The lights went out for a few seconds but came back on.

"A chaplain…? Who put you up to this? This is a horrible joke to play on someone Christmas Eve." Victoria opened the door wider. "Come inside."

The troopers cautiously filed in behind her.

"I'm telling you this is a mistake." She stalked over to the couch, where a Christmas sweater-clad man snored. "Allen Parker is right here. Does he look deceased to you?"

The two men looked at each other. One slipped a cell phone from his pocket and stepped outside.

"Ma'am. I'd like to verify your husband's identity. Would you please show me his ID?"

Victoria walked around the sofa and leaned over her husband. "Allen?" She shook his arm. "Allen?"

He shifted and yawned. "I'm not asleep. Just resting my eyes."

"You were snoring. But there are some state troopers here to inform me that you're dead."

His eyes popped open. "What?" Allen swung his feet off the couch and twisted his neck to see the trooper looming behind him.

"Mr. Parker, would you show me your ID please?"

Allen blinked and shook his head. "I'm sorry… I don't understand…"

"The DPS thinks you're dead. Show 'em your driver's license so they'll go away."

He stood and pulled the wallet from his back pocket and retrieved his ID. The officer took it and scrutinized it carefully, looking back and forth between Allen and the card several times.

Then he photographed the front and back with his phone. "For the file," he said as he handed it to Allen, who reinserted it into his wallet.

Victoria turned to the trooper. "Now that you've scared us half to death, is there anything else you need?"

"I'm very sorry for the misunderstanding, ma'am. Merry Christmas."

He turned toward the front door and Victoria followed to let him out. She held it open for a moment as he rejoined his partner on the porch. "You guys, um, have a Merry Christmas, too. Be safe out there."

"Yes, ma'am. Thank you."

She watched them walk down the drive and get into their car. *Will the neighbors think we're dangerous criminals now? Not-so-confidential informants?* She chuckled.

"What's so funny?" Allen came up behind her and peered over her shoulder.

"Oh, nothing. Now that you're awake, you want some more eggnog?"

He grinned. "I'll get the brandy."

❄ ❄ ❄

Victoria rang the bell on her parent's front door. Her mother, Sylvia, opened it and gave both Victoria and Allen vanilla-scented hugs. "Come on in! Nat'll be here soon."

Allen picked up the heavy bag of gifts and they crossed the threshold. While he added to the package pile under the tree, Victoria made her way to the kitchen. She helped herself to a decorated sugar cookie from a tray resting on the countertop.

She smiled as she chewed. Sylvia's holiday skaters stood on a glass disk about four inches in diameter that was surrounded by resin snowbanks. Victoria picked it up and turned it around until she found the key. As she wound the clockwork, she frowned at the tiny figures. She set it down and watched the skaters glide over the glass to a tinny Christmas carol, their metal skates drawn by magnets that moved underneath the thin sheet of glass.

"Hey, Mom?"

"Yes, baby?" Sylvia pulled a casserole out of the oven.

"Did you get another set of ice skaters?"

Sylvia scrunched up her face. "No. Why do you ask?"

"Maybe... maybe I'm just out of sorts from what happened last night. But I was sure they wore red and green. These guys are blue and yellow."

"That's the set I've always had." Sylvia shrugged. "But what happened last night? Is everything all right?"

"Yeah. It was weird. Two DPS troopers came to the house to inform me that Allen had been killed in a car crash. But he was asleep on the couch."

"That is a very odd mistake to make. Would you take the tea bags out of the pitcher and start filling the glasses?"

"Sure, Mom."

Allen wandered into the kitchen. "Anything I can do to help?"

The doorbell chimed.

Sylvia smiled. "You can answer the door. I'm sure it's Nat."

Allen headed to the foyer. The door opened. There was silence for a moment, then a male voice said, "Are you going to just stand there, Allen, or let us in?"

"Uh... of course. Come on in."

Victoria followed her mother out of the kitchen.

"Oh, Nat! It's so good to see you and Chris," Sylvia threw her arms around the man, then the blonde woman who stood next to him. She knelt to hug a shy toddler who hid behind her mother's skirt.

Allen caught Victoria's eye, and they shared a look of confusion.

"Sis!" Nat swept Victoria into a bear hug. "So good to see you!"

Then he hugged Allen while the blonde hugged Victoria.

"Great to… to see you, too," Victoria stammered.

It seemed that her sister Natalie and her husband Christopher were now her brother Nat—Nathan? Nathaniel?—and his wife Chris. Christina, perhaps?

Victoria slipped over next to Sylvia. "So, where's Dad?"

Her mother scowled, then put her palm across Victoria's forehead. "Have you hit your head? You know your father passed two years ago. You were at the funeral."

"I'm sorry. I—things have been weird lately."

At this point, Victoria was fairly sure she was dreaming. It was a nice enough dream, except for that. Feasting. Family. Festivities.

After Victoria and Allen climbed up the stairs to their room, she paced in a small 'U' around the bed.

"Allen? When did my father die?"

"Well. We just saw him at Thanksgiving. I mean… your mom said two years."

"How is my sister—who was my sister at Thanksgiving—now my brother? How could I possibly get that wrong? Am I losing my mind?"

Allen snorted. "Our minds."

Victoria whirled and caught the edge of a bookshelf. Some children's books fell to the floor. As she picked them up, one caught her eye.

"Allen? Look at this." She waved a book at him.

"What am I looking at?"

She pointed to a banner on the cover. "This says 'The Bernstein Bears.' Stein, with an 'e.' Don't you get it?"

"No."

"It's the Mandela Effect. You haven't heard about that? The main example is that many, many people remember the books as the Bernstein Bears. But they're really the Berenstain Bears. Now, some people just chalk it up to a faulty memory. But others say it's a clue we're on a different timeline. It shifted somehow, and we didn't notice."

"But this doesn't say 'stain.' What does that mean?"

"I'm not sure. Maybe… maybe we're back on the original timeline? Or a different one, except Bernstein didn't change to Berenstain. I don't know. More likely, this is all just a crazy dream that I'll tell you about in the morning."

He opened his arms, and she buried her face in his chest. After a long moment, Victoria pulled away. "I don't understand what's happened. If it's a dream, I'll just wake up and everything'll be back to the way it was. If it's not a dream, and we somehow managed to get on a different timeline, I'm so, so grateful it's one where you didn't die in a car crash. Maybe the whole 'Christmas magic' thing is real."

"Maybe it is."

❄ ❄ ❄

Allen smiled up at the ceiling in the dark, Victoria's breathing deep and slow beside him. Was Christmas magic at play? Santa had certainly brought him a gift. If he didn't die in that car crash, it meant… it meant a lot of things.

Maybe his plan was still in place. He'd been patient, so very patient.

Two years ago, he'd upped both of their life insurance policies from $100,000 to $2 million. He did both so it wouldn't look suspicious, and he'd waited two years to make it difficult for anyone to connect the dots.

Victoria would be out exchanging and returning gifts the day they returned home. He'd just loosen the restraining bolt on her seatbelt and the lug nuts on the front left tire before she got on the freeway and let fate take its course.

After the funeral, after he collected the insurance payoff, he'd slip away to Vietnam with Angelina. Oh, Angelina, with her dark eyes and darker hair. He'd spent the entire delicious morning with her the day he'd been reported as a traffic fatality.

Allen had rented an apartment and had been stuffing a bank account in Hoi An for the last two years. With that and the two million, he and Angelina would live like royalty in a tropical paradise.

A tropical paradise with no extradition treaty.

❄ ❄ ❄

It was the blurry week between Christmas and New Year's and Allen unzipped his coat a few inches. Victoria had sent him out with Gordon—Sylvia's dog—for a walk in the nearby park. She'd insisted, and he needed to get out, so it was the perfect opportunity for him to make sure his preparations were still in place. He grinned as he logged out of the insurance website. In this timeline, the policies were worth $3 million. Then he tried calling Angelina, but it rolled to voice mail. Allen sighed and slipped his phone back into his pocket.

It was a lovely day, sunny and cold. The dog stopped and hunched up his back. Victoria had pressed a roll of pooper-scooper bags into his hand before he left, but he pretended he didn't have any. Now that he'd checked his plans, he wanted to hurry up and go back inside the house. There had been some armed robberies in this park lately. Several people had been shot and one died. He *should* be okay in the broad daylight, but he didn't want to risk it any more than he already had.

A man in a knit hat and sunglasses approached him, his jaw opening into a wide-mouthed grin. "Allen? Allen Parker?"

"I'm sorry. Have we met?"

"Victoria sends her regards."

By the time Allen realized that the shiny thing in the stranger's hand was a gun, he already felt the first bullet searing into his chest.

To explore more content from Artemis Greenleaf, A.B. Richards, and Holly Dey, please visit BlackMareBooks.com